THE WEEDLESS WIDOW

THE WEEDLESS WIDOW

DEBORAH MORGAN

Thorndike Press
Waterville, Maine USA

Chivers Press
Bath, England

This Large Print edition is published by Thorndike Press®, USA and by Chivers Press, England.

Published in 2003 in the U.S. by arrangement with
The Berkley Publishing Group, a member of Penguin Group (USA) Inc.

Published in 2003 in the U.K. by arrangement with the author.

U.S. Softcover   0-7862-5599-4 (Paperback Series)
U.K. Hardcover   0-7540-7327-0 (Chivers Large Print)
U.K. Softcover   0-7540-7328-9 (Camden Large Print)

The text of this Large Print edition is unabridged.
Other aspects of the book may vary from the original edition.

Set in 16 pt. Plantin by Al Chase.

Printed in the United States on permanent paper.

British Library Cataloguing-in-Publication Data available

Library of Congress Cataloging-in-Publication Data

Morgan, Deborah (Deborah A.)
    The weedless widow / Deborah Morgan.
        p. cm.
    ISBN 0-7862-5599-4 (lg. print : sc : alk. paper)
    1. Antique dealers — Fiction.   2. Fishing lures — Collectors and collecting — Fiction.   3. Kidnapping — Fiction.   4. Large type books.   I. Title.
PS3613.O744W44 2003
813'.6—dc21   2003050954

To Loren

Come live with me, and be my love,
And we will some new pleasures prove
Of golden sands, and crystal brooks,
With silken lines, and silver hooks.
                              — John Donne
                                   "The Bait"

And to my mother, Betty Morgan,
for a lifetime of unconditional love and support,
and for the childhood fishing trips.

ACKNOWLEDGMENTS

The author extends earnest thanks to the following people who contributed expertise and support during the writing of this book, and takes responsibility for any mistaken interpretation of the answers and guidelines so generously provided:

to my son, Kevin Williams, for introducing me to exotic fish and raising questions about those in this book, and to Donna Hatch, part owner of University Aquarium and Pet Shop, Ann Arbor, Michigan, for willingly providing answers to those questions;

to Kym Williams, B.S.B.A. and D.A.U.G.H.T.E.R., for marketing consultations, astute suggestions for the manuscript, and the B&B vacation amidst an astounding collection of antique dishes;

to my grandson, Dylan Ray Brown, for teaching me to look at things with eyes of wonder;

to John Lee and the National Woodie Club for their enthusiasm and their willingness to accept Jeff Talbot as the first fictional member of their organization;

to Vicky Loyd, co-director of the Northfield Township Library, Whitmore Lake, Michigan, again, for tracking down reference books and sources of elusive quotes; and to Ron Loyd (the other half of the Loyd co-directorship), for going above and beyond the call of duty when I most needed it;

to writers Noreen Ayres and Robbie Robbins for generously opening their Seattle home and for introducing me to some of their favorite Washington sights;

to Laurie Wagner Buyer, one of the finest poets of her generation, for her friendship, generosity, and inspiration;

to writer Randall Platt for answering all questions asked, no matter how insignificant they might have seemed, and to Randi's "good buddy and fishing freak," Greg Stacy, for providing much valuable information on Washington fishing. Although Jeff Talbot found a different fishing hole from the one sanctioned by Greg, I'm nonetheless indebted to him for the suggestions and the literature;

to Ted Zgrzemski, woodie owner and restorer, and fellow Michiganian, for lending his knowledge and expertise so that I might

better portray Jeff's '48 Chevy;
  and to my husband, Loren D. Estleman, for keeping me grounded and for teaching me how to soar.

PART ONE

THE CAST

ॐ

"An excellent angler, and now with God."
— Izaak Walton
The Compleat Angler,
1653–1655

CHAPTER ONE

❧

Fishing can be an important connection between generations, as well as a way to practice good stewardship.
> — *Washington State Department of Fish and Wildlife*

Her legs were long and curved and dark as bronze, with smooth knees and slender ankles supported by tiny, delicate feet.

Jeff Talbot gazed at her and sighed. She looked better than she had in years and, although the cost had been high, it had been worth it.

She had seven sisters in varying stages of disrepair, but the one standing before him now was the first to have received a face-lift.

The eight matching Chippendale-style chairs were fashioned of mahogany, with cabriole legs and bow-shaped crest rails.

The chairs weren't actually period pieces from the latter half of the 1700s, but rather Victorian Revival antiques, so Jeff's path didn't lead him to the nearest *Antiques Roadshow* taping or to any of the top auction houses of New York. Instead, he took them to a man who was a veritable magician with antique furniture. That man had coaxed to the surface the original integrity of the first chair, and he would easily do the same with the others. It didn't matter that the chairs were 100 years younger than the style from which they'd been copied. Jeff predicted that they would be more valuable than last year's Pontiac.

His discovery of the eight side chairs had been a right-place-right-time circumstance. But his acquisition of them had come years later.

He'd happened upon a pack rat of a woman — ancient, even back then — coming out of a neglected, abandoned-looking house. Jeff approached her, explained that he was an antiques picker, and inquired whether she had any old items she'd like to get rid of. She'd told Jeff that she lived next door and used this extra house for storage. She'd gone on to explain that she had neither the need nor the desire to sell anything. When Jeff had glanced in the direction she'd indicated as her residence, he'd seen a house in roughly the same condition as the abandoned one. Although he had finally gotten the old woman to accept his business card, he hadn't expected anything to come of it.

The phone call he'd received, announcing her death and asking if he might still be interested in "all this junk," had come from a benefacting grand nephew (the sole survivor, it turned out) who couldn't wait to be rid of the contents so he could have the structures razed and a prefab erected in time for the holidays as a surprise for his wife and kids.

Jeff had moved swiftly, scanning the contents of the two houses and offering a price for the lot. The new owner's eyes lit up like Christmas bulbs, and Jeff scratched out a check.

He'd felt as if he'd unearthed a stash of presents, each with a gift tag that read, "Happy Holidays, to Jeff." It was the best deal the picker had made to date.

He'd taken the chairs to Sam immediately upon discovering the distinctive marks that told him who'd originally crafted them.

Now, Jeff turned his attention back to the chair that stood before him. "Sam," he said to the craftsman who'd renovated the piece of furniture, "you've outdone yourself. She's as beautiful as she must've been when your great-great grandfather made her nearly a hundred fifty years ago."

Sam Carver beamed, his teeth blindingly white next to his dark skin. Like many middle-aged black men, Sam had a quality of perpetual youth. In fact, he was five years older than Jeff's thirty-eight. Sam was lean, with arm muscles strung tight from years of carving and sanding and buffing the fine woods of the world. He was a fourth-generation woodcarver and restorer. After the Emancipation Proclamation, Sam's ancestors had chosen to use their vocation as a last name, rather than their former master's surname.

Sam's talent as a restorer had earned him accolades from customers on both sides of the Atlantic. The foundation for those skills had been handed down from eldest son to eldest son along with the tools of the trade.

Those antique tools commanded a higher insurance premium than the building in which Sam worked. By Jeff's estimation, the hand tools alone — planes, clamps, and vises with elaborately etched brass fittings, rosewood handled chisels and carving tools with warm patinas created over decades by the firm grips of craftsmen — would cost

16

more to replace than a blue-collar worker might earn in a year.

Over the years, Jeff had been aware of his friend's desire for a son, the fitting offspring to carry on the family business. And he'd seen Sam's concern increase as each and every one of the wood-carver's five offspring had come swaddled in pink. Fortunately though, Sam's middle girl, Maura, had taken to wood carving like a duck to a decoy. She'd practically grown up in Sam's shop and had officially joined the business when she was sixteen. That was ten years prior — and in the past decade, the Carver business had tripled.

Jeff nodded appreciatively. *Yes,* he thought, *Sam's forebears would be proud.*

Sam rubbed his hands on a once-white rag, which now showed various shades of furniture stain, then stroked the chair's curved back as if she were a lover. "The old gal just needed the touch of a good man, Jeff."

"Don't let Helen hear you talk like that. She'll suspect you've got some young thing on the side."

Sam laughed. "My woman knows she's the only two-legged female I can handle. She's got nothing to worry about."

Jeff turned serious. "We're lucky, you

know. At least our wives appreciate what we do for a living. Some women don't care whether the competition has two legs or four. Or none, for that matter. If they're not the center of attention, then they're jealous."

"Got someone in particular in mind?"

Jeff raised a brow. "That obvious, huh?"

"Only because I've heard that tone before."

Jeff leaned against the bead-board counter. "I've been thinking about Bill Rhodes. You missed our last fishing trip, so you haven't met his young bride." They'd be seeing Bill later that afternoon when they stopped at his bait shop for fishing supplies.

"Bride? Hell, I'd about forgotten that he had one, let alone a young one. Robbed the cradle, did he?"

"Looks that way. Which wouldn't matter, if they seemed like a match. But this one acts like she'd scream bloody murder if a live fish got within fifty feet of her."

Sam raised his brows. "Yeah, well I bet she doesn't bat an eyelash when she sees the bank deposits. That place is a gold mine."

Jeff nodded. Bill's store, the Northwest Territory Bait and Tackle Shop, was a big success, thanks in no small part to Bill's uncanny knack for predicting where the best catches could be made. It didn't matter whether you were fishing for cutthroat, chinook, Dolly Varden, steelhead, coho — whatever your game, Bill Rhodes had your game plan.

In addition, Bill had the state rules for his region memorized. With trout, it was easy and it rolled off Bill's tongue like a tape recording: "Catch-and-release except up to two hatchery steelhead may be retained." Then, he would add, "That's year-round, of course." Rules for salmon were trickier, but he had those committed to memory as well, right down to that tiny window of time during which you could actually keep a chinook.

Sam swiped at a speck of dust on one of the chair's arms. "Reckon she'll try to keep Bill from playing poker? I've been counting on winning a new rod and reel from him this trip."

Jeff noted a touch of Sam's native Southern drawl in his speech. It only happened when the transplanted Texan had had a few beers or was comfortable with the company. Jeff considered it a compliment, and enjoyed hearing an accent in his homogenized Washington. It was a fascinating combination of good-ole-boy and ebonics. "What do you need a new rod and reel for?

Your Bamboo Bomber catches more than a dozen of those new combos would." Jeff and Sam had nicknamed the bamboo rod, which had been a present from Sam's mom to mark his thirteenth birthday, then gave it every possible chance to live up to the moniker during Sam's stays with Washington relatives.

"Now, that depends," said Sam. "You can't figure Gordy's replacement into that. That kid might have the corner on beginner's luck."

Gordy's replacement, Jeff thought. Nobody could replace Gordon Easthope, especially someone half his age. Besides being one of the FBI's top agents, Gordy was, by Jeff's estimation, the best fisherman this side of the whaler Jonah. Gordy had been Jeff's mentor, best friend, father figure, you name it, since their early days together with the Bureau. Contrary to workplace statistics, the two had remained tight after Jeff's sudden departure from government work a half-dozen years before.

"The Judge thinks this kid will be a natural, if he can take his enthusiasm down a notch or two."

"This kid," as Sam kept calling him, was Kyle Meredith, a young attorney who'd been pestering Judge Richard Larrabee to include him in his monthly poker games. According to the Judge, Kyle had recently become hooked on fishing (so to speak) after watching *A River Runs Through It*, and the Judge decided to include him when Gordy had to cancel at the last minute. This, the Judge had said, would give Jeff and Sam the opportunity to get to know the young attorney and see what they thought about including him in the regular poker games.

"So, what do you think?" Sam prompted. "Will Bill be in the games?"

"Hard to say. He showed up last time, but watched the clock like a kid out on a school night."

"You see there?" Sam said. "Much as I love Helen, I'd never take her with us. A man just can't be himself on a fishing trip if there's women around."

Jeff investigated a mahogany table showcased near the chair Sam had restored. They were a remarkable match. "Hell, Sam, you'd better not let some women's libber hear you."

"Too late."

Jeff looked up at the new speaker. Maura Carver walked in through a back door. She'd succeeded in sounding upset, but her smile gave her away. Her bronze skin and delicate features put Jeff in mind of the newly refinished chair.

Maura gave Jeff a quick hug, then turned to her father with a loving but warning look.

The warning appeared not to have registered. "See there, Jeff? Can't even speak my mind without one or the other of my brood eavesdropping. You don't know how lucky you are that Sheila can't traipse along after you. Sometimes I wonder how the hell I've survived all these years with six women under foot."

"Dad." Maura squeezed her father's arm and looked at Jeff apologetically.

"It's okay, Maura," he said. "That's just your father's way of apologizing for his good fortune. If I didn't think he knew how damned lucky he is, I'd have decked him a long time ago."

"Damn, Jeff, she's right. I didn't mean anything against Sheila by it." For a brief moment, Sam's expression hinted at pure self-admonition. Then, without any indication of a shift in gears, he returned to a quasi-irritated state of being overrun by members of the opposite sex. "It's just that our fishing trips are my only chance to get a break from all these women, and missing out on the last one has surely taken its toll."

"We'll fix that in a few short hours," said Jeff.

His thoughts drifted to his own home life. Only a handful of people knew about his wife; fewer still knew that she was agoraphobic. The early stages of her illness had been present when they'd met. It hadn't mattered to him then, and it didn't now. In retrospect, however, he had to admit that the day-to-day challenges were different from what he'd imagined. But he was crazy in love with Sheila, and constantly surprised that so young and beautiful a woman had ever given him a second glance.

Every relationship has something, he told himself. His wife's terror of leaving the house was less traumatic than any number of other demons they might have had to face.

"Jeff?" Maura touched his arm, bringing him back to the present.

"Yes?"

"Are you okay?"

Jeff smiled. "I'm fine." He nodded his head toward the table. "You're tempting me with this, aren't you? It's a great match for the chairs."

"You've got a good eye, and good instincts. Someone has to market all the stuff that Dad takes on barter."

"I figured you were the driving force

behind the success of this place."

Sam grimaced. "She's plenty aware of that without you reminding her."

Jeff studied the table more closely. "Can you hold it for me till we get back Monday?"

"Sure thing," Maura said.

Jeff checked his watch. "If I don't get on the road to —"

"Stop right there!" Sam clamped his hands over his daughter's ears. "That fishin' hole is the only secret I've got left from this brood of females, and I'll be damned if you're gonna take that from me."

"You're right. A true angler doesn't reveal the location." He grabbed the door-knob. "Are you sure you don't want to ride over with me? There's plenty of room in the woodie for your gear."

"No can do," Sam said. "I promised this one she could leave early today, since she's gonna hold down the fort while I'm gone."

Maura smiled. "Sorry, Jeff, but I'm holding him to it. And if he doesn't stop complaining, his *brood* will go to a NOW meeting instead of shopping."

Sam appeared to give this some serious thought. "Honestly, I don't which would cost me more."

A victorious Maura disappeared through the back.

Jeff told Sam he'd see him later at the cabin, then headed out the front door.

The backseat of Jeff's 1948 Chevy woodie was virtually always removed to make room for his antique finds. Today, the back was full of fishing gear, duffel bags, and lidded plastic bins of food.

Most people Jeff's age, it seemed, used their station wagons to haul children, beach toys, and soccer players, a noisy cargo. But Jeff's passengers were always silent, and he wondered sometimes about what he was missing. He and Sheila had agreed not to have children. Sheila had worried that, if her condition never improved, she wouldn't be able to attend school plays, sporting events, recitals. In the beginning, Jeff had argued with her about it, but as he watched her withdraw more and more from the world, he realized that she'd been right.

Today, they'd parted on good terms, despite the fact that Jeff had felt guilty for leaving her. He hardly ever thought about it when he left every day for work, but to leave for a long weekend of fishing with his friends seemed selfish somehow. Sheila had assured him that she had more than enough to keep her busy.

The cleaning crew would be in on Friday. Although Greer, the couple's butler, was in charge, Sheila voiced her belief that as mistress of the mansion she had a certain responsibility to at least look like she was the person in charge. While Sheila relied heavily on Greer to run the household, Jeff had come to depend on the young butler's comforting presence, which made it much easier for the picker to spend hours away from home in order to earn the money it took to keep everything running smoothly.

Fortunately Jeff had inherited the home — although some would argue that inheriting the huge Victorian on Seattle's Queen Anne Hill was *bad* fortune. Funds well beyond a typical mortgage payment were earmarked for the cleaning, maintenance, taxes, grounds upkeep, and a dozen other daily requirements of the fifteen-room monstrosity. But Jeff had grown up there and had been taught to care for the place as if it were a member of the family.

Sheila's weekend, as she'd laid it out to Jeff over breakfast that morning, would be busier than his own. She planned to experiment with some new recipes, make a little "shopping trip" to the personal antique store she had set up for herself on the third floor, and go antiquing at her favorite on-line auction houses.

All this proved that, as usual, she seemed

more adjusted to the situation than Jeff was. That was fine with him, less for him to be concerned about. He found this train of thought reassuring, and filed his concerns about leaving his wife comfortably in a mental drawer under "secured" so that he might turn his focus toward his driving.

He headed toward the waterfront. On the way, he decided to stop by Blanche's. He would have just enough time to get to the docks before the commuters started stacking up at the landings. Besides, he thought, he'd have plenty of time for reflection tomorrow morning on the river.

CHAPTER TWO

൪

SPEAR FISHING: Attempting to take fish by impaling the fish on a shaft, arrow, or other device.

— *Washington State Department of Fish and Wildlife*

Jeff parked the woodie, choosing a spot at the empty end of the large parking lot that paralleled Blanche's antique shop, aptly called All Things Old. He'd recently had the car's wooden finish revarnished and was more protective of it than usual.

It felt odd, going into Blanche's establishment empty-handed. Usually, he had *something* to sell to his favorite client, even if it was nothing more than a shoebox full of vintage hatpins for Isabelle's, the segment of Blanche's store that she'd lovingly named after her three-greats grandmother, and which showcased vintage clothing, shoes, gloves, parasols, chatelaines, dressing table accoutrements, crocodile handbags, and hundreds of hats. The massive collection represented every era in female fashion from the French courtesans to Rosie the Riveter.

Jeff didn't underestimate the value such a hatpin collection would represent. He'd learned a thing or two from Blanche, and one of them was that authentic hatpins were bringing a pretty penny nowadays. There were three kinds of fakes, near as he could recall: reproductions, which as the name implied, were replicas of period pieces; marriages, in which the head and the stem were joined; and fantasies, which weren't like anything from period. But a shoebox full of bona fide antique hatpins had the potential of fetching three or four grand in today's retail market — depending, of course, on the size of the shoes.

He spied Blanche's assistant, Trudy Blessing, talking with one of the cashiers behind the immense, L-shaped counter. As Jeff approached her, he knocked on the polished oak.

She looked up and smiled. "Mr. Talbot, this is a surprise! Mrs. Appleby said you were leaving today for a fishing trip."

"Eventually." Jeff had tried for quite a while to get the young woman to call him by his first name, but hadn't succeeded. Finally, he'd realized that although Trudy was nearing thirty, her quiet demeanor (along with her glasses that made her look like a female Harry Potter) never would've allowed her to pull it off.

Jeff cleared his throat. "Sorry to interrupt, ladies. Is Blanche in her office?"

The women exchanged glances. Trudy said, "No, she's out back at the loading dock. You'll never believe what she just bought."

"What's that?"

"We've been sworn to secrecy. But I *will* give you a hint." She produced a pith helmet from beneath the counter.

"Whatever you say, Miss Blessing." Jeff put on the helmet and both women laughed. He gave a proper British salute like Michael Caine in *The Man Who Would Be King*, then headed toward the back of the building.

Blanche Appleby's voice echoed in the rafters as Jeff approached the unfinished portion of the building. Blanche had been renovating the warehouse for almost ten years, ever since the death of her husband, George. She and George had owned three warehouses along Elliott Bay, and Blanche, not wanting to remain in the import/export business, had renovated the largest and turned it into an antiques mall to rival all antiques malls. She used another warehouse for storage and was currently toying with the idea of giving the Edgewater Inn a run for its money by converting the third warehouse into a posh hotel.

Blanche was methodically calling out orders like an air-traffic controller. Curious, Jeff picked up his pace, turned the corner, and almost ran into the rough-skinned trunk of a taxidermied elephant.

"Blanche?" Jeff shouted over the grunts and cursing of the movers, the squeaking of dolly wheels under the pachyderm's feet (not a full-grown tusker, but rather a youngster the size of a Brahma bull), and the general pandemonium of another dozen men unloading crates from an eighteen-wheeler's trailer. "Blanche, have you lost your mind?"

"Jeffrey?" A tiny woman with coppery hair peeked from around the elephant's trunk and grinned. "Isn't he just *adorable?*" She patted the calf's side as she walked toward Jeff. "I felt so sorry for the little guy that I couldn't just turn him away."

"Turn him away? Blanche, it's not a stray puppy."

"Where's your sense of adventure, Jeffrey?"

"I'm as adventurous as the next guy, but all of us combined don't hold a candle to you."

"The timing was perfect. As you know, I've been working on this corner of the building. I predict that the safari craze is with us for a long time to come, so I bought out the inventory of a New England shop that's going out of business because of the owner's poor health.

"Anyway, this section will be called Burton's, in honor of the great adventurist, Sir Richard Burton." She stood tall and proud, which brought her up to her full height of five feet.

"That means you'll have editions of the *Kama Sutra* in here then."

Her face turned as red as her hair. She slapped his arm playfully.

"Anything in the collection that I'd be interested in?"

"Have a look-see. There's everything you might imagine: skin rugs — lions and tigers and bears —"

"Oh, my."

Blanche continued obliviously. "There are trophy heads to display on the walls: lions, wildebeasts, and giraffes, and there's vintage stuff: leather trunks and cases, that great Campaign furniture that folds up — chairs, beds, desks, tables in all sizes. Mark my word, Jeffrey, Campaign pieces are about to become very popular again, what with the state of this old world. You've seen how popular anything and everything patriotic has become, right?"

Jeff nodded. There was no doubt that America as victim had profoundly stirred the patriotic emotions of everyone worthy of U.S. citizenship. Those who had allowed Jeff to go through old trunks and boxes in their garages and attics had quickly grabbed from him the *Uncle Sam Wants You!* posters, the military uniforms and the foot lockers that had once seen the shores of Normandy and the dust of San Juan Hill, the pennants and flags embroidered with fewer than fifty stars.

All this, of course, had made prices skyrocket. Those things that *were* available in the antique shops and malls across the country were being snatched up in dizzying numbers, and the patriotism of buyers wasn't discouraged by jacked-up prices. They simply dug deeper into their pockets and bought. And bought. And bought.

Blanche went on. "The furniture will be next. People will want anything and everything that might allude to our country's fights for independence. Which leads me to a question: Do you think your recently acquired loot has anything that will fit either my Burton Room, or the Americana Room?"

Jeff grinned. He had worked out a barter plan with Blanche for the use of her warehouse; in return, she would get first pick of the treasures. "You're calling in that marker pretty quickly, Blanche. I haven't stored a single stick of furniture in your warehouse yet." He retrieved a spiral-bound notepad from his jacket pocket and skimmed its contents.

Blanche said, "That can't all be from those two buildings, can it?"

He showed her the cover. It read, *Building One — Residence.* "The only things I've removed are the chairs I told you about that Sam's working on and a couple of items for Sheila's shop. I've told the movers to start with the house where the old gal had lived. It'll be easier to empty — the other is stacked to the ceiling in some rooms — and that'll give me more time to pack up everything in the other one. I have to say, it goes against my better judgment to leave on this fishing trip."

"The break will do you good. You've been working on that inventory day and night for a week."

34

"I suppose you're right. But leaving means I'll have to do the same thing next week when I get back."

"If I can keep up with all this —" she made a grand, sweeping gesture "— then you can inventory two little houses." She tapped on the notebook. "Now, find me some Campaign furniture."

"Here's something." He pointed to a passage written in a form of shorthand left over from his days with the Bureau. It read *CW: c. tent, 6 ch., 2 dsk — 1 wr. 1 slt., all m., x.*

She shook her head. "I'll never get used to your covert note-taking, Mr. FBI. Plain English, if you please."

"Sorry. It means that I have a Civil War era canvas tent, rolled up next to a stack of break-down furniture — the x means legs which fold, a typical design of Campaign furniture, as you know, so it could be compacted and moved easily while on campaign — six chairs, a writing desk, a slanted desk — that one was probably for maps — all made of mahogany."

"Are they in good shape?"

"Near as I could tell. There wasn't enough space to get a real good look at the tent, but the rest of the stuff is in excellent condition."

"Good enough for me. I'll tell Joe and

35

Mark to load them last so they can drop them off here." Jeff nodded. He had asked Blanche to recommend the best movers she knew, and she'd gone ahead and lined them up for him.

"This will add a great feel to Burton's, don't you think?"

"Right up his alley." Jeff put away the notebook, then told Blanche to give Sheila a call if she needed to get in touch with him while he was gone.

He drove on to the ferry that would take him away from the city. As the transport made its way across the choppy waters of Puget Sound, he poured a cup of coffee from his Thermos and began reading a book on American antique furniture. It was an area he wasn't too well versed in, and he needed to brush up because of his recent acquisitions. He supposed it made sense that the two packed houses seemed insignificant to Blanche — hell, she owned the largest antiques mall in Washington — but he wouldn't kid himself. He had his work cut out for him: finishing inventory, wrapping hundreds of glass items, boxing up books, and making sure everything was moved before the demolition crew showed up on the thirtieth.

He'd tacked on a bonus, getting the woman's nephew to throw in fixtures and fittings. The extra money and time would be worth it for the clawfoot tubs and pedestal sinks, stained glass windows that were works of art, etched brass doorknobs and hinges.

Occasionally, he looked up at the diehards standing on deck in the steady mist. They were straining to see land, as if the act would help speed the progress of the big hauler.

When at last it docked, Jeff carefully drove the woodie up the ramp from the belly of the boat and onto the landing. He hoped he hadn't used poor judgment in driving the wood-paneled station wagon. But the forecasters had predicted that the rain would stop by early evening, and he'd decided to put his faith in them. Conditions should be perfect for fishing throughout the weekend.

He headed west toward Bill's shop. He wanted to stop there first to pick up supplies and find out whether the Judge had arrived yet. Richard L. Larrabee, prominent Seattle district court judge and owner of a large fishing cabin, had been the host of this annual fishing trip for the last dozen or so years. Although Jeff had a key to the cabin, he'd prefer that the Judge arrived first to open up the place.

Jeff thought about the Judge's recent announcement to run for governor and wondered whether he would still be called "the Judge" if he won. The man seemed a natural to join the state political arena. He knew the law like Josiah Wedgwood had known jasperware, and besides, his integrity had been well known for decades.

Jeff's thoughts turned to the young man named Kyle Meredith whom the Judge had invited for the weekend. He wondered whether this Meredith kid collected anything, whether he would take up collecting antique lures and such, just as the Judge and Gordy and he himself had. Jeff had always been surprised that Sam *didn't* collect fishing paraphernalia. He had some stuff, but only because he'd never been one to let go of money for something similar to what he already had. If a lure caught fish, he used it — whether it was a glass-eyed plug from the 1940s that had come in the tackle box passed down by his father, or a two-year-old plastic number that Helen had put in his Christmas stocking.

Collections are borne of interest, whether it's an interest generated by a favorite hobby or sport, or by an intriguing object that catches one's eye. Quite often the interest is generated by one's own name — like the woman he'd once met named Virginia Rose, after Homer Laughlin's dish designs of the same name. That woman had more pieces of china than she could count during a leap year. Jeff estimated the collection to be worth in excess of seven grand.

Jeff thought again about Kyle Meredith. He wouldn't have voiced his concerns out loud, but privately he questioned whether an attempt to replace Gordy was necessary. He suspected that Bill would join in the nightly poker games, bride or no bride. And he was a little surprised that the Judge would give a newcomer directions to his secret fishing hideaway. Hell, maybe he planned to blindfold the guy and escort him in under the cloak of darkness. Jeff would've laughed, but in all honesty he wouldn't have been a bit surprised if the Judge did just that.

If a true fisherman knows anything, he knows this: Fishing is serious business.

Jeff turned off the main road and started down the winding gravel lane. Ancient evergreens lined the path that led to the lakefront property where The Northwest Territory Bait and Tackle Shop stood. The building was partway down the slope that led to the dock, beyond which was a huge expanse of water.

Jeff wasn't the diehard fisherman that his buddies were, but the sight of it all calmed him, instilled a certain level of peace that he'd never found anywhere else. The picture before him seemed to promise that time would stand still, trophy fish would leap into creels, and poker hands to make even the most skilled of Vegas dealers nervous would be dealt. The sparkling-water beer commercials were right about what called to a man.

Up top was a large gravel parking area, where Jeff spotted the Judge's old Bronco. The brake lights glowed red like a traffic light against the drab green of the beat-up vehicle, then went dark. He could have replaced the Bronco several times over, but he maintained that his fishing luck would go south if he changed anything more than the sparkplugs and oil. The Judge climbed from inside and turned at the sound of Jeff's approaching car. The tall, slender man waved, then leaned against the wind coming off the lake while Jeff brought the woodie to a stop.

The Judge had white hair — it had been that way since his twenties — and Jeff suspected he used it to his advantage to reflect that seasoned look of a politician. But the older man now fought to maintain a healthy, youthful look by staying tanned and in shape.

Jeff hopped out of the woodie, grabbing a jacket from the front seat. The two men exchanged a warm handshake, then started down the hill toward the shop.

"Is that a Caribbean tan, or a canned one?" Jeff asked.

The Judge laughed and slapped him on the back. "You think I never go fishing but what you're invited? This is pure Washington sunshine."

"I'm surprised you've had time to enjoy what little sunshine we've had."

"I figured I'd better squeeze in some fishing now, before the court docket and the campaign totally take over my life."

"I hope this wind dies down." Jeff shoved his arms into the jacket. "Could play hell with the morning's catches."

"That's for sure, and I'd hate to think we came up on Thursday for no reason."

"I know what you mean." Jeff was glad he made his own hours. "Nothing like catching a good mess of fish on Friday morning, while the working class is stuck in the I-5 corridor."

"Actually, I'm working on some solutions to Seattle's traffic problem."

"Are these solutions about helping your

fellow man, or are you just looking for a way to get the city's votes?"

"Why not both?" The Judge smiled.

"Good point."

Gusts of wind targeted the primitive rockers on the porch of the bait shop, setting them in motion and causing them to creak eerily.

"If this keeps up, all we'll catch on the river is pneumonia," the Judge said with a shiver. "And, I'll be damned if I'm going to subsist on Carver's chili all weekend, just because the fishing weather is lousy. Maybe I'd better buy some extra venison chops from Bill while we're here."

"We should be fine. The forecasters predict this will give up the ghost by midnight."

"That's a sure sign we're in for trouble." The Judge chuckled, then turned the conversation back to the traffic problem while the two walked down the hill. Jeff was so caught up in this information that he uncharacteristically opened the bait shop door and walked in without first scanning the room.

"Good God." The Judge grabbed Jeff's arm.

Jeff stopped, took in the sight before him.

The shop looked liked the Atlantic after a shark's feeding frenzy. The aquarium had been overturned, shattered. Several fish were scattered across the floor, some flapping and jerking pitifully, while others, motionless, stared blankly.

The tank's water had mingled with red liquid and had worked its way across the wooden floor, blanketing the boards with a pinkish tinge. In the center of the room, surrounded by an astonishing amount of blood, lay Bill Rhodes.

CHAPTER THREE

᠅

GEAR RULES: You may not use drugs, explosives, or poison that may kill or injure fish and wildlife.
— *Washington State Department of Fish and Wildlife*

Jeff rushed to Bill, checked his neck for a pulse. If there was one, it was so faint that he couldn't separate it from the one pounding in his own ears.

The Judge reached across the counter for the phone.

"Wait," Jeff said. "Use your cellphone. No sense muddying up the crime scene with our prints."

The Judge pulled back, then nodded and unclipped the phone from his belt.

Jeff carefully rolled Bill onto his back. Right away he saw that resuscitation was out of the question. Blood plastered Bill's shirt, and he couldn't distinguish ripped fabric from ripped flesh.

On the floor where he had fallen lay what looked like a miniature of the devil's pitchfork. Instinctively, Jeff's gaze went to the wall behind the counter, where the antique three-pronged fish spear had hung for the past five years.

"Make it damn quick," the Judge snapped. He punched a button to disconnect the call, then turned toward Jeff.

Jeff saw the blood rush from the Judge's face as his gaze fell upon the body.

"You okay, Judge?"

He shook his head. "I've never seen so much blood."

"I thought you'd be used to stuff like this by now. You've been a judge for years."

"Not *this* side of the crime circuit. Crime-scene photos aren't the same as the real thing." He ran to the back room. Jeff heard water running and wondered if the sight had made the man sick. After a moment, though, the Judge returned carrying an aquarium half full of water. He was red-faced and the veins stood out on either side of his neck. The tank held a jumble of sculptures and treasure chests, and its sides were heavily coated with mineral deposits, but it

45

didn't appear to be leaking. The Judge set down the tank, scooped up a pair of gloves from an overturned display stand, shoved his hands into them, picked up a flopping fish, and placed it in the tank. Then he stooped to pick up another fish.

Jeff walked to where the Judge was working, nodded in the direction of the body. "Looks like it hit his heart."

The Judge straightened and said something about needing more water. He started toward the back, then stopped. "Hell," he said in a hushed tone, "whoever did this might still be here."

"If they were, they'd have coldcocked you when you went back there the first time."

"I suppose I *was* taking a chance. It honestly never crossed my mind that we might be in danger."

Jeff wondered if the Judge had fallen into a false sense of immunity to the underside of the world. That could be as dangerous as a cop who felt untouchable for no reason other than the presence of his uniform and gun.

The fact was, Jeff realized it hadn't crossed his mind either that someone might be lurking back there. He chastised himself for that one. He'd been away from the Bureau for a little more than six years, and although he'd worked the milder side — tracking leads on thefts from museums, libraries, and auction houses — he'd still been *trained*, for God's sake. He'd gone through everything from firing range qualification to cyber-crime strategies. He'd even taught some of the classes at Quantico. Was his new vocation — which consisted of tracking leads on other people's castoffs, shooting through traffic in order to arrive at an estate sale on time, interrogating sellers over the finer points of their wares — making him soft?

He looked at the scene in front of him through different eyes, then said, "We're probably okay. If this had been premeditated, the killer likely would've brought his own weapon. This looks like your classic crime of passion. He probably panicked, took off as soon as he realized what he'd done."

Jeff mentally replayed their movements, not only for his own curiosity but also for the report he knew they'd have to give to the officials once they arrived on the scene. "I don't think we've disturbed things too much."

He looked around. Although this was a bait shop, Bill had obviously invested a fortune in *atmosphere*. The appeal of the place was in its woodsy aromas: jerky in aged barrels, coffee percolating on the potbellied stove, cured-willow creels appointed with leather, alderwood-smoked salmon. Most guys who trekked across land and water to retreat into cabins and tents threw over the daily ritual of scraping stubble from jawlines, the constant headache of commuter traffic, the perpetual stress of corporate America. Walking into Bill's shop was like passing through The Bronze Door. It allowed one to leave everything else behind.

Only the aquarium stocked with exotic fish might have seemed out of place to a stranger. But in Bill, Jeff recognized a kindred spirit: although he liked rugged surroundings, he also enjoyed owning things of beauty.

The Judge cleared his throat, bringing Jeff back to the present. "How long do you reckon he's been lying here like this?"

"Hard to say. Not too long, I don't think, but I could be wrong. The blood loss was fast, and some of the fish were still alive." Jeff watched the fish in the tank. If he didn't know better, he'd say they looked a bit startled, but basically okay. In today's PC society, he wouldn't be surprised if someone suggested bringing in a trauma team for the finned survivors. He shook his head before

48

that picture took root in his brain.

He remembered Bill's cold skin. "Anyway, the M.E. will have a better idea of how quickly a body cools when the blood has gone from it like that."

Jeff looked toward the back of the building. He knew from prior visits that the back room was about a third the size of the retail portion of the shop, with shelving for extra stock and an L-shaped kitchenette in one corner. Another corner held a tiny bathroom. They needed to secure the bathroom.

If the murderer had gone out the back door, he could have bolted in any one of three directions and become immediately hidden by the dense woods. To the west, the fourth direction, was the lake.

"Guess we'd better take a look, huh?" Jeff started toward the stockroom. The Judge followed, and, carefully, they checked between rows of shelves, then threw the bathroom door open with a bang and peered inside. No one.

It took less than half a minute to secure the rooms. When they were through, Jeff looked out a window over the kitchen sink. The wind was still gusting, whipping tree branches and making frothy whitecaps on the lake's surface. "If they left by way of a boat, they had a challenge on their hands."

The Judge looked over Jeff's shoulder. "I sure as hell wouldn't want to be out there."

"He, or she, had a lot —"

"She?" The Judge's tone was heavy with skepticism.

"Could've been. Although she would have to be one hell of a strong woman to thrust a spear that far into Bill's chest. Anyway, the killer had a lot of choices for someone who didn't plan ahead. Could've escaped by boat, or car, or even on foot, for that matter. Lots of remote cabins out here."

The back door was standing open and the screen was unlatched, but Jeff knew this was nothing to be alarmed about. Bill had always kept it unlocked during business hours for people coming in off the water.

He opened the door, careful not to touch anything. He and the Judge went out back to check for any clues that might tell them if the killer had left that way. There were several different footprints on the dirt path that led up from the dock, but the last hour's drizzle had played hell with their definition. No telling how many people had been in this morning, or how many of the tracks belonged to Bill himself, who had often boated over from his home on the opposite side of the lake.

Instinctively, Jeff glanced toward the

dock, scanning the area for Bill's boat. It wasn't there. Bill's truck hadn't been in the parking lot, either. Jeff wondered whether Bill's truck or boat had been stolen, or whether Tanya, Bill's new wife, had dropped him off. It wouldn't have been the first time Bill had been a victim of theft. He'd had a break-in a couple of years earlier and had lost several antique lures.

Just then the distant wail of sirens came from the south.

Jeff and the Judge walked around the building and stepped up onto the porch as the sirens grew louder and louder. They choked off with a squawk like that of a bird grabbed by the throat, then two uniformed officers made their way down the path from the parking lot.

"Don't touch anything!" A portly, ruddy-faced boy waved his arms as if he were fighting flies off a pie. "You hear me down there? Don't touch a damned thing!"

"Simmer down, Roy," said a woman's voice behind him. "They either have, or they haven't, and there's not a blessed thing you can do about it now." Jeff picked up a slight hint of an Irish brogue.

Roy's complexion reddened further — an angry shade — but he didn't say anything else.

As they neared the porch, the second uniform circled around the hefty kid. "I'm Sheriff Colleen McIvers. This is my deputy, Roy Manning."

Sheriff McIvers had a creamy complexion, green eyes, and what might have been red hair had there been any under her tightly cinched ball cap. Chemo, probably. A closer look revealed telltale signs that she'd lost some weight, too. The wind lifted her unzipped jacket to reveal loose-fitting slacks held up by a belt showing previous wear a good two inches looser than the current notch.

McIvers stepped over the threshold of the bait shop. "Lord, this place looks like a slaughterhouse. What happened, Bill," she said to the victim as if he might actually answer her, "did you go and miss a fishing prediction and get somebody's ire up?"

She squatted beside the body, checked the neck with her fingers.

Jeff said, "I couldn't find a pulse. Are you getting anything?"

The sheriff frowned. "Have you got some kind of training?"

"The FBI kind. In my former life."

"That means you don't know crap about murder." She took a notepad and pen from her pocket. "What's your name?"

Jeff introduced himself, letting the sheriff's comment ride. True, FBI agents didn't investigate murder except in special cases, but they damn well knew how to check for a pulse.

"Who's your sidekick?"

The Judge's face showed an unmistakeable look of disbelief at the woman's lack of professionalism. Nevertheless, he extended his hand so quickly that Jeff figured it was a new habit his friend had practiced for the campaign trail. "Richard Larrabee."

"You look familiar." The sheriff shook the Judge's hand, all the while studying his face.

"Newspapers or television, perhaps. I recently announced my intention to run for governor."

The sheriff's brows arched slightly, but she gave no response. She scribbled something else in the notebook, then turned to Roy. "Use the cruiser's radio and get Gary out here. Tell him to call Lester, too."

"Yes, Ma'am."

"And stay up top," she added. "Keep the gawkers and would-be customers out of here."

The sheriff studied the crime scene for a few seconds. She walked around the counter, punched a cash register key with a pencil eraser, and grunted once. "Didn't come for the money."

Jeff said, "Or else they got scared away before they could get to it."

She looked at him, but didn't respond. She nodded toward the body. "Who turned him over?"

"That would be me," Jeff said. "I'd hoped I could perform CPR, but . . ." His voice trailed off.

"You secured the back of the building?"

"Yes, Ma'am."

"What all did you two touch?"

Jeff spoke first. "I only touched the body. The back door was open. I pushed against the screen with my shoulder."

She looked at the Judge expectantly.

"Ah, I opened the front door when we arrived. Anyone would've done that. Used my cellphone to call in — that was Jeff's idea." He indicated the fish tank. "Then I got this aquarium from the back, put on some gloves, and picked up the fish that were still alive."

Jeff heard a commotion, then two paramedics rushed in on either end of a clattering gurney and almost fell when the soles of their shoes hit the wet floor.

"Take 'er easy, fellas," the sheriff said.

"There's nothing you can do here but wait for Mills to show up."

They conducted a perfunctory exam anyway, and the sheriff didn't seem to mind. Everyone had a job to do.

After they'd determined that there was no hope for Bill, the men parked their gurney out of the way and stood beside it.

The sheriff said, "I wonder how long it takes for a fish to die."

"What?" Jeff asked.

She indicated the motionless fish on the floor.

All four men shrugged.

"We're in a fishing village, for Pete's sake. Don't tell me nobody knows how long it takes for a fish to die." She shook her head, then furiously scribbled on the notepad.

One of the paramedics pulled a pack of smokes from his jacket pocket, gave a jerk of his head to his partner, and the two of them went outside.

After they'd left, Jeff indicated the wall. "You might want to make a note that the murder weapon is an antique. It was taken from that empty spot in the display."

"And how would you know that?"

"For starters, I sold it to Bill. I'm an antiques picker. I buy —"

"I know what a picker does, Mr. Talbot."

The sheriff jotted something in a notebook as she spoke. "He buys from the poor and sells to the rich."

The Judge nudged Jeff. "She's got your number, Talbot."

The sheriff turned back to Jeff. "So, you know a lot about the murder weapon, Mister Picker?"

"There are good and bad in every profession, Sheriff," Jeff said. "Even yours."

"Point taken."

"As far as the murder weapon goes, I just know that it's antique. Vintage, anyway. Type of thing Bill liked."

The sheriff started out the door. "You two come with me."

She went out on the porch, positioned one of the rockers opposite two others, then told the men to sit. They sat.

"I'll be back in a minute." She walked around the building, and Jeff figured she was looking for more clues. She was back in less time than it took to tell it. She dropped into the chair facing them, wrote something else in her notebook, then looked up. "Give it to me from the top."

Jeff picked up on the fact that she sounded a little out of breath. He wondered how she kept up with the demands of her job. Of course, murder investigations ran few and far between out here.

It didn't take him long to give her a rundown of the afternoon's events, and to tell her that an initial check of the scene revealed nothing much in the way of clues. Of course, he'd missed the relatively obvious fact that no cash had been taken.

"Which one of you is driving the classic?"

"That would be me," Jeff said, wondering if he'd have to trot out that phrase a third time before they were through. He also wondered if the question was relevant.

"What are you? A surfer relocated from California?"

"No. I like the water, but not from on top of a board. Actually, the woodie's great for hauling the loot I get from those people you think I'm putting in the poorhouse. And when I *really* clean somebody out, I send in a couple of muscled-up bouncer types with a big truck. Besides, the woodie generates more trust than if I were driving a beat-up old truck and wearing last week's castoffs."

She watched Jeff a moment, then smiled. "Do you own a fishing cabin up here?"

"I do." The Judge cleared his throat. "But, what makes you think we're here to fish?"

The sheriff laughed. "You're wearing flannel instead of robes, driving a Bronco instead of a Jaguar, and stopping at a bait shop instead of the county courthouse in town. I could've deduced that when I was twelve."

The Judge arched a brow. "Well done, Sheriff. Is this where I'm supposed to offer you a job with my campaign?"

Jeff detected a flicker of something in the sheriff's eyes as she stared at the Judge. Resentment? "Thanks just the same," she said finally, "but I like being a hick in the sticks. I may not work too many homicides, but nothing says I can't handle it."

The Judge's expression relaxed. "I have no doubt that you can."

Jeff thought how frail the sheriff looked in the large wooden chair. It hadn't crossed his mind to question the abilities of Sheriff McIvers. He offered an observation in hopes that it would get the questioning back on track. "Murder is murder, Sheriff, and the fact that this one happened in a relatively isolated fishing area doesn't change the ripple effect. I don't envy you your job."

The sheriff nodded without comment, then said to the Judge, "Where is your cabin?"

"At the end of Gordon Road. My friends" — he nodded toward Jeff — "and I come over whenever we get the chance."

"Friends? I only see one."

Jeff said, "Two more will be arriving this evening."

The sheriff started writing again. "How do you know they aren't already in the area?"

Now, there's a good point, Jeff thought. To the sheriff, he said, "I left one of them at his workplace in Seattle —"

"And I did the same with the other," said the Judge. "Matter of fact" — he checked his watch — "he had a deposition to give about forty-five minutes ago. There's no way he's here yet."

The sound of tires crunching gravel came from the direction of the parking lot. A few seconds later, two men and a young woman made their way down the path.

"I only heard one car," the sheriff said as she stood. "What'd you do, Gary, carpool?"

"Sure, why not? Lester here was at the station when Roy Boy called."

Jeff noted that Gary's build was enough like "Roy Boy's" to have made them brothers. This one was several years older, but the two shared the same red face and portly build. The man referred to as Lester, thin and gray haired with rimless glasses, carried a black metal case. Jeff figured him for the M.E.

"Paramedics are out back. You can give them a holler when you're ready for them." The sheriff sent the trio inside, then spent the next few minutes getting contact information from Jeff and the Judge. Once she finished that, the sheriff announced that she'd better go break the news to Bill's wife. "Have either of you met her?"

"Yes, actually," Jeff said. "We met her last year, briefly. Didn't really visit with her, though. We'd just bought supplies and were leaving when she dropped by the shop."

"That's right," the Judge said. "Bill was happy as a clam, showing her off to us. There was no mistaking that."

Roy, who had walked back down the path, snickered at what he'd obviously over-heard. "I bet that was the last time she was here at the shop," he said. "She's usually gone shopping, or with her personal trainer, *Gunther,* or out on the golf course, or trying to get Bill to agree to that real estate deal, or —"

"Roy." The sheriff's voice sounded strained. "Get back up top and keep this place secured."

"I came down to tell you that —"

"Wait," Jeff said, unable to contain his curiosity. "How would you know her schedule?" He half expected the sheriff to remind him just who was in charge of investigating this murder.

"That's easy," said Roy. "My mom is Tanya's hairdresser."

"Roy," the sheriff said, "didn't anyone ever tell you that you can't believe a damned thing a beautician says?"

Jeff wondered if her attitude had something to do with her own lack of hair.

The sheriff jotted something else in her notebook, then looked at Roy. "Do what I told you and keep the area secured." She leaned in to deliver the next line to the deputy. Still, Jeff caught the words loud and clear. "And that includes your mouth."

The M.E. walked out onto the porch, stripped the latex gloves from his hands, and deposited them in a zip bag. As he sealed it, he said, "Rain's picking up, Colleen."

"So?"

He dropped the sealed packet into a pocket of his lab coat. "So, uh, shouldn't you get inside somewhere before you take sick?"

She glared at him. "I meant, what about Bill?"

"Don't have to worry none about him getting sick." When she gave him a warning stare, he turned to Jeff and the

Judge. "Sorry, folks. It's that laugh-to-keep-from-crying ploy. I'm gonna miss that ol' coot."

Jeff suddenly realized that he would, too. Bill was as much a part of the scenery there as the lake and the evergreens and the fish themselves. The place would never be the same without him.

Lester was still talking to the sheriff. "Looks like he bled out. That, combined with the cold water all over the floor kind of throws a kink in the guessing game. Offhand, though, I'd say he's been dead three, four hours."

The M.E. took a deep breath, then continued. "See if you can find out whether he went home for lunch, or brought something here with him, or stopped down to Rhonda's."

A picture of Rhonda's Café came to Jeff's mind. It was a little hole-in-the-wall down on Main Street that still had its chrome-trimmed red and white Formica and vinyl from the fifties. Some of the best food in Washington, though.

The M.E. went on. "I'll get the autopsy going, but it might speed things up if we can find out about his lunch hour. Let me know if you dig up anything." He stepped off the porch, then turned, blinking against the rain. "Meant to ask, what's with all the dead fish on the floor?"

The sheriff filled him in, concluding with the question of the day.

"Damned if I know from fish outta water, Colleen. Might ought to check with a pet shop, or at the library, or someplace like that. There's a pretty good sized aquarium at that new Chinese restaurant down by the ferry docks."

"I'll do that," she said. "Right now, though, I'd best get over to Bill's house and notify next of kin." She fished a couple of business cards from her shirt pocket and handed them to Jeff and the Judge.

The young woman who had arrived with the two men — Jeff figured she was the detective's partner — began unrolling police tape and started wrapping it around the porch posts. She looked like a stick figure, right down to the large round head with squiggly hair all around, like a child would draw.

"Save yourself some trouble," said the sheriff, "and do that after they get the body out."

The young woman blushed, then set the roll on the porch floor and went inside.

"I'm through with you two for now," the sheriff said to Jeff and the Judge. "If you think of anything else, well, you know what to do." She wrapped her jacket tight around her thin frame and hurried up the hill toward the parking lot.

Bill's house, the sheriff had said. Not *their* house. Jeff considered this, but then realized it was probably a common mistake. Bill had lived alone for a lot of years after his first wife died. His current wife had most likely had a hell of a time being accepted by the residents of this close-knit community.

Jeff recalled his first impression of Tanya Rhodes. A sensuous, platinum blonde bombshell. Kaboom, for most red-blooded American men. Marilyn Monroe without the hips. Yet although he was as warm-blooded as the next guy, Jeff wasn't turned on by that much silicone. He had to admit, though, he wasn't blind to it, either.

Women had many options, and all were appealing to one or another type of man. Some women still subscribed to big hair, acrylic nails, spike heels. Others sported a more streamlined, yet equally appealing natural look. Like Sheila: blonde pageboy cut, nicely shaped nails with no bright polish or extensions, the classic build of a young Katharine Hepburn.

To each his own, but he felt compassion for Sheriff McIvers. He couldn't completely say what it was like for one female to be intimidated by another, but he couldn't help wonder how the scene would play out as the news of Bill's murder was delivered to his beautiful young widow.

Sheriff McIvers could handle it, Jeff was sure. But his heart went out to the bald woman named Colleen who dwelled inside the gaunt, uniformed body.

CHAPTER FOUR

All fishing gear must be kept in immediate control and may not be left unattended while fishing. Rodholders may be used; the rod must be easily removed without delay; rod may be left in holder while playing the fish. Downriggers may be used if the line releases from the downrigger while playing and landing the fish.

— *Washington State Department of Fish and Wildlife*

Jeff pulled a knob on the dashboard, and the woodie's headlights shot beams through the veil of drizzle and illuminated the wet pavement. There should've been another hour of light, he thought as he made his way to the cabin, but the gloomy weather was gobbling it up like a trout greedy for the evening's hatch.

For the first time in living memory, Jeff had bought supplies from a store in town instead of from Bill Rhodes.

After Sheriff McIvers had released them, Jeff and the Judge had climbed into the woodie and worked on a plan.

They'd practically shouted over the rain, the woodie's canvas and slat headliner magnifying the downpour, while Jeff had scratched out a grocery list of items that would make a cardiologist choke: milk, butter, bacon, eggs, sausage, cheese.

The Judge would go on to the cabin to open up, get a fire going, and wait for the others to arrive, while Jeff backtracked into town for the supplies.

The shopping trip had taken longer than he'd expected. He had called Sheila from a pay phone on the side of the market's building to let her know that he'd arrived safely, and had given her a brief version of the afternoon's events. When he concluded, he received a lecture about protecting himself.

"I'll be fine, hon," he said after his wife trotted out all the typical rules. "My skills may be rusty, but there's still enough 'agent' in my blood to save my skin if the need arises."

"Just be careful. I haven't traveled with

you for a few years, but I still remember how distracted you get when you're on the road. Whether it's for a fishing trip, or antiquing, or even going to the corner store, you're always searching for something you can buy and resell, always scoping out places where people usually store stuff. Just remember to watch your back, okay?"

"I promise." Jeff watched while a woman with a bag of groceries on one hip and a toddler on the other struggled to open her car door. He wondered absently whether the young mother was aware that a murder had taken place near here only a few hours earlier. "Actually, though," he said to Sheila, "no one in town acts concerned. I probably won't even hear anything else about it, unless there's a funeral while we're still here. I'm telling you, honey, it's an isolated case. Just one of those things."

"Right. Random act and all that. What happened, J. Edgar? Decide to forgo the 'motive' portion of triptych?"

Jeff bristled. He usually didn't mind when Sheila alluded to his days with the FBI, and he actually liked her nickname — triptych — for the three constants in a non-serial murder: means, motive, and opportunity. But he hated it when she tagged him with the Bureau founder's name. It meant that she didn't believe he was taking things as seriously as he should. "What do you say we finish up this call before I come up with a choice nickname for you?"

"Sorry, Jeff. I just needed a little interaction, I guess. Figured if I riled you, you'd stay on the phone longer."

Was she trying to make him feel guilty for being gone? That wasn't like her. "I thought you had your weekend without me underfoot planned down to the minute. What happened?"

"Oh, I do. I'm just restless, I suppose. Greer just left to meet Robbie at the Seattle Center to see a new production, and . . . I don't know, the house seems emptier than usual."

"What about painting?"

"I tried. It came out as gray as the weather."

"What about going on-line? You could scare up someone in your group."

"Tried that, too, but no one's there." She laughed, and he picked up on the ironic tone in it. "Can you believe that? It's not like they've all gone out to dinner and a movie. We're agoraphobic, for God's sake. You'd think *somebody* would be at his damned computer."

Jeff sighed. "Don't tell me they have lives,

too? Sheila, honey, think about all the things you do that aren't directly tied to the Internet: cook, read, paint, keep journals, develop recipes, research. And, when I'm there, we watch movies and, hell, you were working out alone in the basement gym before I joined up. You could do that. My point is, others do all that. Maybe you're not the only agoraphobe who leads a relatively normal life."

"You're right." She sighed. "I'm sorry."

"Why don't you go shopping? My treat."

"I suppose I could. It wouldn't hurt to start thinking about Christmas."

He cringed, not from the thought of outgoing money, but from the mention of a holiday that was still over two months away. He decided it was a female thing, to shop and plan and make out menus and wrap gifts and decorate. The list went on and on. For him, it only served to rush the year's end and eat up the weeks. Nonetheless, he delighted in what the Internet had done for his wife. Shopping was now an option, thanks to an ever-increasing list of dot-com stores.

"Oh, shoot," Sheila said, "I forgot to tell you. Blanche called, said she needed to talk to you about the warehouse. I'm sorry I didn't mention it earlier."

"That's okay. I'll give her a call when

we're through." He thought for a moment. "Hey, why don't you invite Blanche over?"

"I'm one ahead of you. She's coming for dinner tomorrow night. I'm going to make my apple and squash soup."

"Now that's something you could've sent with me."

"And compete for first place against Sam's famous chili? I'm smarter than that."

"Well, at least make enough for leftovers, will you?" He didn't expect an answer. Sheila knew it was one of his favorites, and now that the leaves were turning, he looked forward to her recipes for hot soups and pumpkin bread and lots of oven-roasted delicacies. His wife's daily baking during the autumn and winter months gave the old house an added coziness. "Speaking of which, I'd better go so I can call Blanche, then get to the cabin before that chili's gone. And you can finish planning your menu for tomorrow night."

"With Christmas shopping to do? Nope, the menu can wait till morning."

"Have fun, honey. Love you."

"You, too, Talbot. Cha-ching." She rang off.

He laughed. She could shop all she wanted, as long as he didn't return home to find a trimmed tree in the parlor.

After his conversation with Sheila, Jeff had checked his watch, then had punched in the phone number to All Things Old. He'd hung up on the recording of Trudy's voice that gave the antique mall's hours and had tried Blanche's home number instead. No answer. No automated anything, either, as Blanche strove constantly to maintain simplicity. Jeff had decided he'd try her later from the Judge's cellphone.

He had spent most of the drive back to the cabin thinking about Bill. Now, he turned his thoughts toward the weekend. Blanche was right, he needed the break to recharge. He grew anxious to join the others and kick back.

He scratched at the stubble on his face. Like anyone serious about snagging game, he'd stopped shaving the morning prior. He'd also skipped applying cologne and had dug out a bar of unscented lye soap that he kept on hand for the express purpose of getting ready for a fishing trip. Some didn't believe that human scent was a warning to fish, just as it was to deer. Others answered that assumption by telling the doubtful Thomas to stick his hand in the water of his favorite trout stream and then see if he didn't plod home with an empty creel. Jeff wasn't paranoid, but he admitted to a little of the Judge's superstitions regarding his old Bronco. Jeff didn't want to take chances by tempting fate, either.

Sheila had grown used to his stubble, his smell without colognes and scented soaps, his sort of pre-fish philosophies before the infrequent fishing trips. Last night had been no different from every night with her before a long weekend of angling, and Jeff grinned now as the image of the previous evening came to mind. In short, she'd lured him by coming to bed wearing nothing but his beat-up old fishing hat and a smile.

After a moment spent savoring that memory, he thought again about how different Sheila was from Tanya Rhodes. While the Rhodes woman was an hourglass with ample sand at the top, Sheila was a Lalique vase, tall and slender, subtly yet gracefully curved, classic, valuable. Both women were blonde, but where Tanya's hair was obviously bottle-platinum, Sheila's was sandy, natural.

He leaned forward, peered up through the woodie's windshield. He hoped the forecasters were right. He would fish in the rain, but he much preferred to cast his line amid bright shafts of sunlight.

Richard Larrabee's cabin was at the end of Gordon Road, named for the old man who'd sold the place to the Judge two decades earlier. Actually, it wasn't a Road with a capital R at all, but a private lane that meandered through a pine forest and opened up on a clearing with a magnificent log structure that looked out over one of the best trout streams in Washington.

Jeff caught flickers of the cabin's lights through the boughs of the evergreens. Smoke from the chimney hung low in the evening's damp weather, and Jeff practically felt the warmth of the logs that he knew waited, banked and glowing, in the massive stone fireplace.

Nothing about the cabin would have changed since last year, he could count on that. Most of the furnishings were simply marking time in order to reach the century milestone so they could cross over that threshold from vintage to antique. It was a hodgepodge assemblage of pieces from the twenties, thirties, and forties — all those things that had been discarded after World War II and replaced with chrome and plastic. Although the purist who stuck to a single style would have cringed, the motley pieces gathered in the Judge's cabin actually worked. They provided a certain comfort, like a well-worn sweater at the end of a damp autumn day in the Northwest.

Oversized chairs and couches looked like a traveling troupe's carpetbags — faded, soft, sagging in all the right places. Jeff sighed. He could sink into the cushions of one of those chairs right now and never come out. Just give him an ancient copy of *Field and Stream* from the stack left behind by the previous owners and a mug of coffee laced with something to warm his bones.

Throughout the cabin were mismatched bureaus, dressers, tables, sideboards — all with marred surfaces, missing knobs, or mirrors in need of re-silvering. The beds — two in each of the two large bedrooms — ranged from unadorned wood to the elaborate wrought iron and brass concoctions that one might have found in a twenties bordello.

The kitchen was U-shaped and large enough for three or four people to work in without getting in one another's way. From the design of the place, Jeff figured it had been built by two couples — probably in-laws — who would have come out from the city on weekends to fish, play bridge, and generally enjoy the state's natural resources.

Surprisingly to Jeff, the Judge seemed quite comfortable at the cabin, although it was a far cry from his elaborate waterfront home in the city's Magnolia neighborhood.

There, the Judge insisted on perfection. Out here, though, as he'd often said, he didn't want to worry that he'd be out too much if the place was ever broken into.

At the Judge's request, Jeff had located smaller items that either weren't antiques or weren't yet *valuable* antiques — things he came across in people's attics, garages, barns, and at yard sales while out picking. He'd made a decent profit providing the Judge with old framed photos of fishers and hunters with their harvests, vintage wooden skis, snowshoes with frayed webbing, creels with missing lids, ugly lamps, wobbly smoking stands, and humidors minus their barometers.

The place had two bathrooms, the only rooms that still hinted at the prior presence of any females. They were identical, each with a clawfoot tub whose exterior was painted a delicate pink to match the pink tile on the walls and floors. Extra lighting around the mirrors spoke volumes about an era when no proper lady stepped out without her lipstick applied just *so*.

To put a masculine spin on the pink bathrooms, Gordy had donated a few vintage fishing posters and advertisements he'd found two decades before at a flea market near Dowagiac, Michigan. Most, Jeff estimated, were from the forties and fifties and were of Varga girls in swimsuits and short-shorts. But the favorite among the men was a rare layout advertising the Heddon Company's Tad Polly lure. In the ad stood a top-less beauty. "Wait till you see my Tad Polly!" she suggested. "It floats — It dives — It dances!"

Yes, indeed. The Judge's cabin was no place for a lady.

Jeff pulled in next to Sam's old pickup out front. On the other side, next to the Judge's Bronco, was a foreign job the size of a bumper car. It was so small, in fact, that Jeff wondered how a driver had actually shoehorned himself into it. And, hell, forget about getting any kind of fishing gear into the thing.

He grabbed the grocery bags and made a dash through the rain for the front porch. Sam swung open the door and stepped out to help with the packages. But, as he did so, a cricket chirped, and Sam was off in search of it like a ten-year-old. Jeff didn't mind, knowing how lucky Sam was when using in-sects as bait.

He stepped inside and met an onslaught of friends and food. The guys were in good spirits, their laughter and camaraderie im-mediately infectious, and the aromas of

Sam's Call-Your-Local-Fire-Station-Chili and jalapeno cornbread made Jeff's stomach growl. The Judge could complain all he wanted about Sam's spicy cuisine, but Jeff had missed Sam's traditional first-night supper last time around.

This year, it was Gordy who'd be missed, and Jeff wondered how the old reprobate was holding up. The older man had canceled by saying only that duty called, then had added that if it continued to cut into his fishing trips, he would take early retirement and fish any time he damn well wanted to.

Gordy's kitchen skills wouldn't be missed, though. Other than frying up a tasty fillet, the man couldn't cook worth a damn. His Departure Stew two years earlier had been an unappetizing concoction of everything remaining in the fridge, and had actually driven the Judge to order pizzas from town.

There wasn't much opportunity for frying fish nowadays, since the sport had gone mostly toward catch-and-release. The group hoped every year for a mess large enough to provide one decent supper, but since hatchery fish were basically the only ones by law that could be harvested anyway, and since the art of fly-fishing was attempted by more and more people, the odds of success had changed.

Jeff's luck had never been that great anyway, and it was usually Gordy or Sam who made sure that one night wasn't spent eating Vienna sausages and crackers.

Other than that, there were certain, predetermined guidelines for the meals during this annual fish-fest. The Judge, who was by nature a morning person, was the breakfast cook; Sam Carver was always in charge of the arrival-day supper and always used recipes passed down by his "Lone Star granny;" Jeff brought along desserts, breads, and home-canned comforts that Sheila delighted in preparing; and, if the group had luck with them while out on the water, they would team up in the kitchen for a big fish fry with all the trimmings — hush puppies, cole slaw, corn on the cob.

Everything that the foursome planned to consume over the weekend was measured in man-words like pounds, slabs, sacks, hunks: ten pounds of onions, three slabs of bacon, two five-pound hunks of hard cheese, three pounds of coffee, a twenty-pound sack of potatoes.

Jeff shed his jacket and poured a cup of coffee.

"I hope you remembered to buy antacid," the Judge said.

"C'mon, now," said Sam, who had returned to his post in the kitchen. "All this sweet-talk where my cooking's concerned is getting to me right *here.*" He slapped his own butt.

The Judge just shook his head and turned away. When he did, Sam upended a bottle of orange-red liquid over the bubbling stockpot. Jeff recognized it as a twin to the bottle Sam had put in a gift basket for Sheila last Christmas. If he recalled correctly, its label said something like Off-the-Charts Habanero Hot Sauce.

"I'll need a stomach transplant when he's through with me." The Judge sighed, then switched gears. "Jeff, I'd like you to meet Kyle Meredith. Kyle, Jeff Talbot."

Jeff shook the young man's hand. "I take it you're the one driving the matchbox car out front."

"The red one? Yeah. How come?"

"I'd like to know how you managed to get more than a toothbrush in there with you."

"Hell," Sam said, "the boy done brought two high-dollar rod-and-reel combos, three tackle boxes, a suitcase *and* a garment bag, two sets of waders — one for backup — and —"

"And nothing," Jeff said. "There's no way he got all that into that car."

"*And* —" Sam leaned on the word — "one of the tackle boxes is *full* of old lures that he wants to get rid of."

Jeff was halfway out the door on his way to unload the rest of his supplies before Sam's words registered. He stopped, stepped back inside. "Old lures? When can I see them?"

The Judge came forward. "*We,* Talbot. I want a crack at them, too."

"What's kept you from going through them already?"

"Carver here reminded me that I'm a judge. 'Fair in all things, upstanding citizen,' you know the spiel."

"You're forgetting the votes, Judge. Or, should I say, *governor?*" Sam held up seven fingers. "And that doesn't even include my no-account son-in-laws. I'll tell you what, it adds up."

"How did you know about the lures, Sam?" asked Jeff.

"Kyle was here when I pulled in. We unloaded everything and waited on the porch for one of you guys with a key to get here. That's when he asked if I wanted any of 'this old stuff,' as he put it."

"It *is* old stuff," Kyle said. "Belonged to my grandfather. Dad gave it to me when I told him I was going to take up fishing." He shrugged. "I didn't have the heart to tell him I'd already bought new."

"Did he ever," Sam said as a timer beeped. He stuck his hand in an oven mitt shaped like a fish, then pulled an iron skillet from the oven. The cornbread's peppers made Jeff's eyes water. "Purtiest stuff I've seen in a long time," Sam went on. "It'll be interesting to see what he catches tomorrow. 'Course, I told him I'm not a collector, but you two could probably get in a regular bidding war over the stuff."

"I don't want any money for them. I just thought somebody might like having them."

"Hell, this guy does have a heart," Jeff said. "Are you sure he's a lawyer?"

"Oh, he's a lawyer, all right," the Judge said, "but he's new at it. Give him some time."

Jeff rubbed his hands. "Where's the stuff?"

"Nothin' doin'." Sam ladled chili into large stoneware bowls. "Y'all can mess with that after we eat."

Jeff started to protest, then remembered that he hadn't eaten since breakfast. "I'll just grab my gear out of the car, since I'm already wet."

He made a quick dash between the cabin and the woodie. When he returned, the three men were seated at the round pine table.

Jeff poured another cup of coffee, then joined them. Sam handed him a basket of steaming cornbread.

"I have an idea." The Judge rubbed knuckles along his jawline, creating a sound like sandpaper on silk. Jeff figured the man's stubble was as scratchy as his own. The Judge said, "Why don't we let Kyle use them as betting money during the poker game?"

"Well now," said Sam, "that would make things right interesting. But you boys keep forgetting that I don't want the damn things."

"Oh, hell, Sam. You never win anyway." The Judge, who'd been scanning the table as if he'd lost his keys, hopped up and went to the pantry where he dug around until he unearthed a bottle of red wine.

Jeff gulped coffee. "Tell you what, Sam. If you win any of them, you can bet them in the next hand. Then, if you happen to have any left when it's time to go home, we'll figure out something. What do you say?"

Sam hemmed and hawed, but finally agreed.

"What about it, Kyle?" asked the Judge. "Does that work for you?"

"Doesn't matter to me, as long as I don't have to haul them back home."

"Okay," Jeff added, "as long as we can figure some way to put a monetary value on them beforehand."

"Why should we?" the Judge asked. "I say it'll make things more interesting, sort of up the ante, if you will. When it's time to bid, Kyle can reach down in that tackle box — carefully, of course," he added with a smile, "and pull out a lure. Then, whoever winds up with them will have made a good deal, and Kyle will go home with his cash still in his pocket.

He looked at Jeff. "After that, you and I can decide whether we want to make any deals, separate from the card games."

"I don't want Kyle to feel cheated."

The Judge blew on a spoonful of chili. "Kyle had law school handed to him on a platinum platter. Believe me, he doesn't need the money."

Kyle just shrugged his shoulders, then dove into Sam's chili as if he hadn't eaten in a month.

The only sounds heard for the next few moments were the thuds of beer bottles and coffee mugs on the table's pine boards and the clunk and clatter of tablespoons against crockery bowls (Sam maintained that nobody could properly eat chili with a flimsy little teaspoon). Even the Judge drank his wine from a stein instead of stemware, befitting the rustic setting.

At length, Sam looked up. His expression was serious. "We haven't talked about what y'all found today." He looked at Jeff. "The Judge filled us in about Bill while you were gone to the store."

"Not much to talk about, really," said Jeff. "At least, not until we find out some more details. Hell of a note, though, isn't it?"

"No doubt about that," said the Judge. "It would've made more sense if the cash register had been empty, or if there'd been some other evidence of theft."

Kyle finished off his beer. "Still could've been theft. Trick is to find out what was stolen. Or, your friend could've been mixed up in something, or with someone. The wrong someone, you know?"

"Nah," Sam said. "I mean, we didn't really know Bill, like seeing him every day, or taking the wives out on Saturday night, that sort of thing. But you know how you just *know* somebody? I can't see Bill Rhodes mixed up in anything shady."

"I have to agree," Jeff said.

"So do I," added the Judge. "But Kyle could be right. What if Bill was involved in something — even something as simple as, say, an extramarital affair?"

Sam grunted. "You call an affair *simple?* You ain't met my wife, have you?" Jeff was aware that the Judge had known Sam and Helen for years. "If she even *thought* I was having an affair," Sam continued, "she'd kill me dead without even *asking* for an explanation."

Kyle laughed, then turned serious. "You mentioned earlier that the victim had a gorgeous young wife. Why would he *need* to have an affair?"

No one offered an explanation.

Kyle continued. "What about this? Maybe the new young wife simply got tired of good ol' Bill and decided to hurry things along. How old did you say he was?"

"*Now* you're sounding like a lawyer." Jeff got up and put another pot of coffee on to brew. He grabbed a stack of saucers from the cabinet, then unpacked an oatmeal pie that Sheila had sent along. "To answer your question, I'd say Bill was close to fifty. Is that about what you'd figure, Judge?"

"Sounds about right."

"And the new Mrs. Rhodes. What would you say? Thirty-one, thirty-two?"

Sam whistled.

The Judge leaned forward. "Do you think she's that old? I would've guessed twenty-five." He fell back in his chair. "Oh, what the hell do I know? The older I get, the younger *they* get. Especially with the miracles of modern technology."

"You're right about that." Jeff dished up generous portions of the pie and passed them out as if he were dealing cards. "All that nip, tuck, add, subtract, color, and buff presents such a *natural* image, doesn't it?"

"Yep," said Sam with no small amount of irony. "You'll never convince me that there's a woman alive who *really* wants to be cloned. Not a damned one of them is happy with how she looks as it is — take my word, I've got six of 'em. Can you imagine how any one of them would react if that were times *two?*"

All four men laughed, then dug in to the pie. After several groans of praise were offered up, Sam was the first to put the compliment into words. "How in the hell do you keep from weighing three hundred pounds? If Helen could cook like this . . ." He paused a moment, then shook his head and went back to eating. It took a lot to render Sam at a loss for words.

"Well put, Sam," the Judge said. "Worth wading through your four-alarm concoctions to get to." To Jeff, he said, "What else did that gourmet chef of yours bake?"

Jeff smiled. Sometimes he suspected that his fishing buddies invited him along just so they could have a little taste of his personal heaven.

Before Jeff could respond, Kyle held out his plate for a second helping. "Your wife's a chef? Which restaurant?"

Jeff hesitated, then took the plate. He hadn't given any prior thought as to whether the Judge would apprise Kyle of his home situation. While he dished up another piece of pie for the young man, he contemplated his answer. How much should he reveal? He and Sheila had an agreement of confidentiality. They kept the particulars of her illness close to the vest — so much so, in fact, that only a handful of friends even knew Jeff was married.

Well. Jeff had to assume that the newcomer was trustworthy. Why else would the Judge include him in the close-knit group? He contemplated for another moment, then came up with a solution.

He placed the saucer in front of Kyle, slid his wallet from his hip pocket, and pulled out a ten dollar bill. "Mr. Meredith," he said, "is this enough to ensure attorney-client privilege?"

"Well, sure, but —"

Jeff held up a hand. "That's all I need to

know." He handed the money to Kyle, along with a thumbnail sketch of Sheila's illness, of her obsession with maintaining a low profile, of her unfulfilled desire to become one of the country's top chefs.

He concluded on an upbeat note. "She's a whiz with the Internet, as you can imagine. It's brought everything to her: friends who don't have to know about her illness, as well as other friends who are also plagued with it. Then, there are the on-line department stores, specialty food shops, bookstores, clothing stores. Even though we have a butler, Sheila —"

"A *butler?*" Kyle, who had been leaning forward, taking in Jeff's story, fell against the back of his chair. "As in 'Fetch my slippers, Jeeves'? Or, 'Draw my bath, Jeeves'? Hell." He slapped the ten spot down on the table. "I should've asked for more money."

"Like I have any. Most of what I make goes toward retaining Greer and the upkeep of the house I inherited. And don't forget on-line shopping."

"Greer. He, or she?"

"He."

"An old man?"

"No. Matter of fact, he's Sheila's age. They're both in their late twenties."

Kyle's brows shot up. "You're kidding, right?"

"No, why?"

"Where do I start? Let's see, how about as a lawyer?" Kyle stood and cleared his throat. "Do you deny, Mr. Talbot, the similarity of your own marital status to that of the deceased and his *young* wife?"

"No, counselor, I suppose I don't." Jeff grinned. He glanced at the Judge and Sam and saw that they were enjoying the exchange as much as he was. This was almost as entertaining as an auction house full of shills.

"Has it not crossed your mind that you possess a particularly naive outlook on your intriguing home life? Are you telling me that you *trust* this 'young' butler with your 'young' wife?"

"No reason not to, counselor."

Kyle Meredith paced the floor, then stopped, placed his palms flat on the table and leaned over Jeff. To the Judge, he said, "Your Honor, this is a clear case of insanity."

"Mr. Meredith?" Jeff waited long enough to make sure he had the young attorney's attention. "Believe me, it's not a problem."

Jeff arched his brows as if to say, *Do you get my drift?*

Finally, the implication sank in.

"Oh." Kyle's face tinged red and he sat back down.

"Case dismissed." The Judge rapped the table with a knuckle.

Jeff said, "I'm glad I retained your services, Kyle. You're not half bad. To tell you the truth, though, I would've hired Greer anyway, and not because of laws against discrimination. He came to us with impeccible references, he's the most devoted employee I've ever known, and his presence in the house gives me total peace of mind about Sheila when I'm working, or —" he spread his hands to encompass the group, the cabin — "taking a break to enjoy the company of friends."

"I never thought about it before, but I suppose it's the same as when anyone's housebound." Kyle looked concerned. "You said it's a big house. Is she able to move around?"

"Sure." Jeff frowned. "Why?"

"A friend in college had an agoraphobic sister. He said she didn't leave her bedroom for months."

"Sheila's very well adjusted to it, thank God."

Yet despite his answer, an alarm of sorts went off in Jeff's brain. What if Sheila got worse and worse until, eventually, she was confined to one room? He couldn't imagine it, frankly. For starters, which room would she choose? She loved to cook, but she couldn't very well start sleeping in the kitchen. She enjoyed sitting in the library with him while they were both reading, she thrived on time spent at the computer or in the northernmost room of the house where she painted or . . . he shook his head. No, there was no feasible way she could do all she loved to do if it got that bad. Surely she'd see that coming, do *something* to prevent becoming such a prisoner in her own home.

Jeff stood, started clearing the table. The others followed suit, and the foursome made quick work of the cleanup, moving like one machine working toward a common goal. Sam washed dishes while Jeff wiped down the table. He tossed a hand towel to Kyle, who took the cue and dried.

When they were through, the Judge headed toward the dilapidated Hoosier cabinet. The finish of the tall, free-standing work center was well worn, its flour sifter was missing, and its enamel worktop had been chipped by generations of farm wives kneading, mixing, and preparing bread and pies for baking. Its drawer screeched when the Judge opened it to retrieve a deck of cards. He broke the cellophane seal. "Counselor," he said with a sly grin, "isn't it about time you showed us that tackle box?"

CHAPTER FIVE

ॐ

TROLLING: Fishing from a vessel while in forward gear making progress under power.
— *Washington State Department of Fish and Wildlife*

"I'll bet a dollar." Sam lifted four quarters from a precarious stack and dropped them into the pot.

The Judge sighed. "You're not going to win the hand anyway, Sam. Why don't you bet that frog you've got caught on your sleeve?"

Sam lifted both arms and found the barbed culprit. "Hell, I keep forgetting about these." He removed the hook from his flannel shirt and exchanged the little lure for a dollar bill.

Nothing happened for seven seconds.

"Your bet, Kyle." Jeff's patience over the past few hours had worn thin. Trying to incorporate the young man's tackle box of lures into the hands had slowed things considerably. After ten minutes into this portion of the evening, Jeff had decided that poker games and collecting didn't mix. In addition, he hated to play cards with someone whose temperament and pace ran more toward a long-distance chess match.

"I'll see your bet and raise you another dollar." Kyle's luck that night had been worse than Sam's, and in front of him the tabletop was almost bare. He reached for the tackle box.

"Uh-oh," he said. "Looks like I'm down to some old boxes."

Jeff sat up. "Boxes? Do they have anything in them?" Anyone who collected knew that an item was worth a lot more if it came with its original packaging. A twenty-five dollar lure could easily become a seventy-five dollar item. He realized that he may have appeared too anxious, and a glance at the Judge confirmed his suspicions.

The Judge grinned. "Forgot you were playing poker, eh, Talbot?"

He ignored the comment, regained control of his emotions. "I'll play what I'm dealt, same as always."

"You'd better hope it's good, if you want to beat these babies." He tapped the cards that lay facedown in front of him. "Especially if those boxes have anything in them."

Jeff turned to Kyle. "How many do you have in there?"

Kyle stood and tilted the tackle box. The smaller boxes inside tumbled to the table like bricks from a wheelbarrow.

Jeff guessed there were fifteen or twenty of them. Most were cardboard, but a few were made of tin. The tin ones would be older and would in most cases command a much higher price.

The Judge whistled.

Jeff started opening the boxes. Each one contained a lure, each like new. Jeff read the names: The Creek Chub Wiggler, The Redfin Minnow, Minnie the Swimmer, Bubble Bug, Tiny Tease. There was one that read, simply, "Victory," in a font that suggested patriotism by incorporating stars into its bunting-like design; the Helga-Devil looked like graduated beads borrowed from a plastic necklace and had a red top like a hat. It had three barbed treble hooks — one like delicate feet, the other two protruding from the body like arms. Jeff wondered who Helga might have been. He figured the cheapest lure would bring around twenty or thirty dollars, the most valuable, five to six hundred.

There were a couple of point-of-purchase displays for Busy Bait, each inner card holding half a dozen small lures. An Al Foss Pocket Kit was unearthed, and Jeff suspected that it alone would fetch a couple hundred dollars if it was intact. He carefully pried open the lid. The contents looked as if they'd never been removed. There were a couple of Shakespeare boxes, too, as valuable as their names were unimaginative — Sure Lure, Revolution, Rhodes Wooden Minnow. They'd be worth — what? — four hundred, easy, Jeff thought. He reached for a box marked Dowagiac something, but before he could focus on it, the Judge stopped him.

"Would you look at this? A Tad Polly! Have a heart, fellas. I've got to put this in the bathroom with our TP poster girl."

Kyle nodded. "Consider it a gift for inviting me out here."

"If I'm not mistaken," Jeff said, "that's worth more than the bottle of Royal Lochnagar that Gordy blessed you with last year."

The gift of single malt Scotch was one of a case Gordy had purchased at auction in Chicago. Story was that the cases had been exhumed from the watery grave of a ship's skeleton at the bottom of one of the Great Lakes.

"Don't mind if I do." The Judge grabbed an old-fashioned from the cupboard and filled it with ice. Pouring the amber liquid, he said, "Bottled heather, as smooth as lamb's wool."

"Can we get back to the damned game?" Sam drummed his fingers on the table.

"Relax," Jeff said. "You'll have ample time to lose." To Kyle: "You've got quite a little fortune here. We can't in good conscience use these in a nickel-ante poker game."

"If you have any better ideas, I'm open to suggestions," the Judge said.

Jeff knew that anyone with an interest in collecting lures had to apply the same patience a fisherman applies while waiting for a strike. The task of identifying acquisitions was time-eating at best. Most lures of the early and mid-twentieth century were produced in series, and each series might have a half-dozen or more color schemes in both wood and spook — or transparent — baits.

He thought of the example he often used for beginners. The Creek Chub 700 Series from that company's 1941 catalog, for instance, was the Famous Pikie Minnow design, with three treble hooks, two on the belly and one at the tail. It could be purchased in several different colors — the hundred slot being the body style, and a change in the ten or one slot being the particular color, i.e., No. 702 was the Pikie Minnow in white with a red head.

Names given to lures ran the gamut from frighteningly masculine — like Torpedo, King Cuda, or Mr. Death — to decidedly coquettish: The Charmer, The Enticer, The Hooker.

There were premonition names like Lucky 13 and Voo-Doo, and names that gave the illusion of either danger (Convict, Dillinger) or dandies (Dapper Dan, Gentleman Jim). Place names were popular, too: the Bayou Boogie, the Florida Flapper, the Colorado Spinner, the Arkansas Trench-Back Popper.

Most of the collectors Jeff was aware of concentrated solely on a sub-category: lures from one company, or lures made only by a Florida company or the ones produced solely in Michigan.

"Guys, it's after eleven," Sam said, interrupting Jeff's mental odyssey. "Somebody do something."

"I'll make this easy." Kyle closed the boxes, piled them in front of him, and with eyes closed separated them into two piles. He opened his eyes and pushed one pile toward the Judge, the other to Jeff.

"A true Solomon if ever there was one," Jeff pronounced.

"What do you say we have a nightcap, then hit the hay," the Judge said. "Five o'clock comes mighty early, even out here."

Sam grabbed a couple of longnecks from the fridge and twisted off the caps, then handed one to Kyle. The Judge poured brandy into a snifter while Jeff poured another cup of coffee, leaving enough room to top it off with Kahlua.

After they'd all taken up residence around the fireplace, Jeff said, "Kyle, the Judge told us how you got interested in fishing. Have you read the story, too, or just seen the movie?"

"You're kidding. There's a book, too?"

This, just when Jeff had started to like the young man. He smiled, then disappeared into the bedroom where he'd stowed his gear. He returned with a copy of *A River Runs Through It* and handed it to the young man. "It's by Norman Maclean, not Hollywood."

"Ease up on the boy, Talbot," said Sam. "The Judge brought him to us in time to give him a proper education."

"Gentlemen." The Judge leaned back and went through the ritual of lighting a cigar. "I expect we'll learn whether or not that's true by how many fish he brings in for tomorrow night's dinner." He threw a challenging yet good-natured look at Kyle.

Kyle quickly finished off his beer, then stood. "I think I'll take this to bed and start reading."

Sam was still fiddling with his pipe — scraping the bowl, tamping in fresh tobacco, sawing a chenille cleaner through the stem's channel. He smoked only on these fishing trips. When Jeff had asked him why he even bothered, he'd gotten an answer that made perfect sense.

"I need something to do with my hands," Sam had said, "when I'm not busy at the shop. Plus, it helps me remember what's in my collection."

Sam had begun his pipe collection by accident. Someone had brought a magnificent sideboard to him for renovation, and Sam had discovered a felt-lined drawer with fitted slots holding a dozen pipes. He'd called the owner — "a sweet little old lady . . . till she opened her mouth," who had exclaimed that it was a nasty habit and she'd always despised her husband for taking it up. She'd told Sam he could throw them in the trash. After working for her, Sam decided that her husband probably had smoked purely out of spite.

Jeff did a little research, declared them to be antiques worth more than the sideboard in which they'd been stored, and advised Sam to hang on to them.

Since then, Jeff had kept an eye out for old and unusual pipes and had helped increase Sam's collection to more than a hundred.

"Damn it." Jeff suddenly remembered his earlier conversation with Sheila. He glanced at his watch. "I was supposed to call Blanche. Couldn't reach her when I was in town."

The Judge motioned toward the Hoosier cabinet. "Use my cellphone, if you can get the damned thing to work out here. Might have to take it out on the porch."

"Thanks." Jeff grabbed the phone, then took it and his coffee outside.

The rain had stopped, and the wind had died down, but it had gotten quite a bit cooler during the time he'd been inside. The hour was late, but he knew Blanche would be up. Sometimes he wondered whether she slept at all.

He punched her home number and waited. Nothing. No ring, no busy signal. He studied the display, decided that the phone wasn't getting a proper signal, or whatever it was that a cellphone needed.

He stepped back inside, put the phone away, and set down his empty cup. "No signal. I'm going to run down to Bill's" — he paused, then continued, "down to the pay phone. Don't wait up." He grabbed his jacket and headed out the door.

As Jeff pulled down the drive to the bait shop, he saw a makeshift roadblock composed of a couple of sawhorses with yellow caution tape wrapped around them. He hoped the law hadn't gone completely nuts and sealed off the phone booth as well.

Headlights shone from the other side of the sawhorses, then he made out the bubbles on top of the cruiser.

"I thought that was your fancy car." Sheriff McIver's voice. She walked up and grabbed one end of a sawhorse. Jeff jogged toward her. "Let me do that." She wouldn't let go, but he hoisted it in the center and was able to carry the lion's share of the weight.

"I came down here to use the phone," Jeff said after they'd cleared the path. "Any chance your assistant stayed away from it with the tape?"

"Here, use this." The sheriff unclipped a

cellphone from her belt. "I can't give you much privacy, but it'll be easier than convincing my deputy down there not to shoot you. Either that, or you'll have to drive into town."

Jeff took the compact-shaped box. "I tried the Judge's up at the cabin, but couldn't get a signal. What makes you think this'll work any better?"

"Has a little booster chip or some such technology planted in it. Damn thing's probably what gave me cancer."

Jeff had started to put the thing to his ear. He paused. "Do you really think so?"

"Who knows? They could probably print the things that *don't* cause cancer on the inside flap of a matchbook." She smiled then, and Jeff caught a glimpse of a twinkle in her green eyes.

He returned the smile. "How'd your visit go with Bill's widow?"

"Typical. Disbelief, followed by shock and then anger. Although I'm not sure if the anger was directed at the perpetrator or her husband."

"Oh? What makes you suspect it would be directed at Bill?"

"She said that he usually came home every day for lunch. Today wasn't any different. But lately, he'd spent more and more time on the computer, and less time with her. She said that she and a real estate agent had needed to talk to him about something important — she wouldn't give me any details — but that Bill had shown up late, then taken his lunch to his basement office and had spent the entire time on the Internet."

"Internet?" Jeff had been to Bill's basement office a couple of times in years past, but he didn't recall seeing a computer setup. "Since when did Bill jump on the technology train?"

"Beats me. But a check of his files at the bait shop turned up quite a few receipts for on-line purchases. Also found some receipts from a pet store in Seattle. I called, talked with the manager. He knows a guy who's really into exotic fish. Said he'll get in touch with him, have him call me. I told him the sooner the better.

"Listen," she concluded, "I'll just sit in my car and fill out some reports while you make your call."

"Thanks."

"Be quick about it, though. I'm beat."

Jeff assured her that he would. Leaning against the woodie's grille, he punched in Blanche Appleby's home number and hit Send.

"Blanche?" he said when she picked up. "It's Jeff."

"Who's Colleen McI?"

"What?"

"I broke down and got caller ID."

"You might as well go all out and get an answering machine, Blanche."

"One step at a time." She cleared her throat. "Colleen?"

"I'm using the sheriff's phone."

"I won't even ask. Anyway, sorry I missed you earlier. I was at the hospital."

"Hospital? Are you all right?"

"Oh, I'm fine. But, Jeffrey, there's been an accident."

CHAPTER SIX

❧

POSSESSION RULES: You may not possess another person's game fish unless it is accompanied by a statement showing the name, address, license and tag number, date, county, and area where it was taken, and the signature of the angler who harvested it.
— *Washington State Department of Fish and Wildlife*

Jeff leaped to his feet. "Oh, God, is Sheila —" *Wait a minute,* he thought, *this isn't making any sense.* Sheila was the one who'd told him that Blanche wanted to talk to him. But what if something had happened since then? That had been — what — three, four hours ago?

"Sheila's fine," Blanche said. "If anything had happened to her, I'd have found a faster way to reach you."

The sheriff leaned out the window of her cruiser, asked if everything was okay. Jeff nodded, waved her off, paced.

"I know, I know." He started again. "Sheila said you needed to talk to me about the warehouse. What's that got to do with an accident?"

"I didn't want to worry her with what happened, so telling her that seemed a safe way to make sure you would call." She sighed heavily. "The boys were coming back into town with a load of your antiques when a car lost control in the rain. The driver cut across the lane in front of the moving van."

"Is everyone okay?"

"Mark is. They admitted Joe overnight for observation, but they said he should be fine in a few days."

"The car?"

"Driver's fine. Mark said it was a teenage girl. She brought the car to a sliding stop, then jumped out and ran across four lanes of traffic to see if the boys were all right. You won't believe what Mark said she was wearing."

"What's that?"

"One of those Space Needle T-shirts someone came up with after the earthquake last February. Says, 'Shaken but not stirred.' "

"I have a feeling we're all going to want one of those." Jeff leaned against the woodie. "How did it all start?"

"Joe swerved to keep from plowing into the car. The doors on the back of the truck popped open, and, as Mark put it, 'furniture jumped outta the back like broncs at a rodeo.' That threw off the balance, and the truck went over on its side. I would imagine the highway department is still cleaning up the splintered mess from the freeway.

"They hadn't intended to go back," Blanche continued, "but Joe's date had canceled on him, and Mark didn't have anything planned. So, they decided to move one more truckload, get a head start."

"Some head start." Jeff was quiet for a moment. "Well, at least the guys are going to be okay. Any idea which pieces were lost?"

"Mark said it was just about everything from what he thought was a music room. He remembered that a piano was in there."

Jeff sank to the woodie's bumper and shielded his eyes with his free hand, as if he could block the image of the ruined antiques — but all that did was give him a clearer vision. The room with the piano wasn't actually a music room, but rather a place where the occupant apparently had stored extras —

anything for which she had no use or no space for in the rest of her home. Jeff fumbled for his notepad. Tilting it into the beam projected by the woodie's headlights, he found the sheet and deciphered the code he'd used to list that room's contents: one oak baby grand piano, excellent condition, no chipped ivories; one couch, one loveseat, both Victorian with original horsehair upholstery; six matching rosewood music stands adorned with ornately scrolled lyres; a stately rectangle George I tallboy, or chest-on-chest, with a brushing slide (Jeff remembered wondering when he saw it whether the pullout shelf to lay clothes on for brushing had given someone the idea for inventing the ironing board); a Queen Anne highboy, truly American with its flame-finialed pediment made from New England maple and pine; one Chinese screen, black and gold lacquer. His list went on and on. The loss was reeling. Sure, he'd be able to collect some insurance money, but the *history* of those pieces? Jeff felt as if three centuries of his small world had been reduced to a pile of kindling on I-5.

"Jeffrey? *Jeffrey?* Hello?"

"What?"

"Are you all right?"

"Sorry, Blanche. Just going over the inventory of that room."

"I know. It's hard to take. It's not like you can just waltz into a furniture store and pick up more, is it?"

"You've got that right." Jeff stood and stretched, as if the act would lift his spirits as well.

"Mark said there were some boxes of smaller items, too. He remembered, because one was marked 'comic books' and he has several from when he was a boy."

"Damn." Jeff sank back to the bumper. "They were in plastic sleeves, but the rain will have ruined them by now." Jeff had found many collectibles in the main house that had seemed more fitting for a boy, instead of the crotchety old woman he'd met years before.

"Well, you're in luck. Mark grabbed the box and took it with him to the hospital. He said he figured it was the least he could do, and he couldn't stand to leave them out in the elements."

"Remind me to give him a bonus."

"I'd say a few of those salvaged books would make him happy." Blanche added, "I know you're on a tight schedule. Is there anything you need me to do?"

Jeff thought a moment, realized the need to move into action. "You know who to trust, Blanche. Of course, I'll cover the costs if there's another team you want to give this to, or if you want to check with the fellas tomorrow, see what approach they want to take. If Mark feels up to it, he can get a replacement for Joe."

"Okay, boss. I'll get on it first thing."

Jeff chuckled. He doubted that Blanche had ever called anyone boss before. "I'll call you tomorrow afternoon and see where we stand."

After they'd said good night, he returned the sheriff's phone and gave her a brief rundown of what had happened. After she'd offered sincere condolences, Jeff realized that both of them were beat, so he told her good night as well, then climbed back into the woodie.

Back at the cabin, he quietly unlocked the door and let himself in. All the lights were off except for a small lamp in the living room and a night-light in the bathroom. The guys had turned in, and Jeff needed to do the same. As the Judge had pointed out, five would come early.

But he knew he wouldn't be able to sleep yet, and, besides, he was still chilled from standing outside. He warmed a cup of coffee on the rangetop, added a splash of Kahlua, then took it to the living room.

His mind swam with questions. Would Mark even feel up to tackling the rest of the stuff this weekend; was Joe up to it or not? If so, what would he move it *in?* From the way things sounded, the truck was shot. Well, Blanche would make sure things got safely back on track.

He pictured the rooms in the two houses, literally brimming with antiques, and wondered again why the old woman had been so intent upon hoarding all that stuff. What purpose did it serve, squirreled away where no one could enjoy it, admire it, care for it, learn from it? But, Jeff chided himself, that was a question for another time. Right now, he was exhausted. Cold, too, in spite of the coffee he'd drunk as a warm-up. He shut off the lights, made his way to the room he and Sam were sharing. Sam was snoring steadily. Jeff changed into a sweat suit and climbed into the bed on the opposite side of the room.

As he fell into a fitful sleep, he couldn't help thinking of the antiques that had been. He also thought about Bill, killed with a weapon from his own collection, and the frail sheriff, still working at midnight in the bone-chilling damp . . .

He awoke the next morning only by the

grace of God and the aroma of strong coffee.

The room was dark, except for the sliver of light along the bottom of the door. He fumbled for the alarm clock, focused on the soft glow of the numbers and hands. The pale green that illuminated the ancient clock reminded him of the jadite coffee cups, mixing bowls, and vases from the forties that were becoming increasingly popular . . . and valuable.

Almost five o'clock. He groped for the lamp's pull chain, got the old thing to kick in after three jerks, and crawled out of bed.

He glanced at the opposite side of the room, surprised to see that Sam wasn't there. Jeff couldn't believe he'd slept through his friend's rising and getting ready for the day.

He crawled from under the warm quilts, dressed in an old pair of khakis, a white T-shirt, and a heavy plaid flannel shirt that had been washed so many times it felt like chamois against his skin, then padded in thick socks down the hallway.

A corner lamp was on in the living room, casting a soft glow. Kyle stood in the middle of the room, surrounded by more fishing paraphernalia than Jeff had seen in Cabela's latest catalog. The kid was looking around his goods as if he didn't know where to start. He refrained from telling Kyle that he didn't need filament clippers, four boxes of flies, the cumbersome net. These were things he must learn on his own if he was to become a fly fisherman. He'd weed out these items as his skill increased, as his love for the sport heightened, as he learned to crave the challenge of taking a fish in as near a state of nature as he could get — on the same level as his quarry.

The glaringly lit kitchen was in full swing. It was open to the dining area like the stage of a theater. The Judge whistled as he chopped onions on a cutting board near the range top. Jeff squinted against it all and made his way toward the coffeepot.

"Good morning, Talbot," the Judge said brightly, throwing a stick of butter into a skillet the size of a manhole cover. The butter spat and sizzled and slid across the surface. The Judge grabbed the handle and shook it as if he were making popcorn the old-fashioned way, then scooped up a double handful of onions and threw them into the butter.

Jeff gulped coffee. "Morning? I'll take your word for it."

"Still a night person, huh? You burn a lot of daylight that way, my friend." The Judge opened a large package of smoked salmon, then began breaking eggs into a crockery bowl.

Jeff took his coffee to the table, where Sam was busy studying a couple of brightly colored flies wrapped in a small suede pouch. He looked up. "You'd best drink that bean juice faster or you ain't gonna be fit for man nor fish." He set the pouch aside and poured orange juice from a pitcher into four squat glasses.

"Yeah, yeah." Jeff took a swig from his coffee mug, then glanced toward the living room. "Think anyone will offer to help Kyle figure out how to strap on all that crap?"

Sam drained one of the juice glasses in two gulps and set it on the table with a thud. "Beats me. I'd like to know how he's gonna manage to stay afloat in the water. But I reckon the Judge can worry about that."

Jeff absently scribbled the letters "FBI" on a notepad, and set about coming up with an epigram in order to get his mind percolating for the day. It was a favorite five-finger exercise that had helped keep him sane through his years with the Bureau. The first one came easy, and he penciled in the noble statement: Fishing Builds Integrity.

Sam pulled the pad toward him, wrote something, and pushed it back to Jeff.

Jeff read: "Fishing Breeds Insanity." He

looked up. "Are you crazy?"

"Put away your toys, boys. It's about time for breakfast." The Judge came from the kitchen, carrying a tray that held ketchup, salsa (obviously a request of Sam's), butter, and an assortment of syrups and jellies.

"Say, Jeff," he added, "I just remembered that you were trying to reach someone last night — that antiques woman, right? Any luck?"

Jeff had damn near forgotten the conversation with Blanche, a sure sign that he needed more coffee. The reminder brought back all his misery of the night before. "Oh, I reached her, all right. But if what she told me is any indication of how my fishing's going to be, I'd do just as well staying here."

"What happened?" Sam asked.

As the Judge went back to the kitchen and finished cooking breakfast, Jeff filled them in on the accident with the moving truck.

Sam, who'd taken in the story with an increasingly distressed expression, was the first to comment. "It pains me to think of all those antiques getting broke up like stove kindling."

"That's how it hit me, too." Jeff drank the last of his coffee. He liked to have at least one cup in him before eating anything, and at the rate the Judge was moving in the kitchen, he figured he'd better down it fast.

"You were insured, weren't you?" the Judge asked.

"Basically. It's not much consolation, though, when you're dealing with antiques. As Blanche pointed out last night, I can't just go out and buy replacements."

"True," the Judge replied, "but it'll help cut your losses."

Jeff debated whether to try and enlighten him, then decided it wasn't worth the energy. He looked over at Kyle, who was about to step into his waders. "I'd hold off, if I were you. It'll be a hell of a lot easier if you rig up just before we head down to the river."

"Thanks." Kyle grinned nervously.

"It's ready, boys," the Judge announced, and the men gathered in the kitchen. Ceremoniously, the Judge bowed and handed each a platter. Jeff loved this part, in spite of his disdain for morning. The fishermen always stuffed themselves with a large breakfast to hold them through a snack-sized lunch and the wait for a decent supper.

They loaded up their plates with smoked salmon omelettes, hashed brown potatoes, red flannel hash, blueberry pancakes, buttered raisin toast, sliced cantaloupe, and broiled grapefruit halves.

The group remained quiet while they ate, save for the initial compliments to the chef.

After they finished and cleaned up, the four men quietly gathered their fishing gear and reconnoitered on the front porch.

Jeff breathed deeply. It was the same every year; there was a reverence about it. Ritual. Tradition. He recalled a phrase from McGuane's book of essays on fishing: the voodoo of rigging up.

At this stage, when they readied for their first trip to the river, Jeff didn't much care whether or not he would catch a fish during the course of the day. He could rely on that euphoric romanticism to continue as he waded into the chilly stream and studied its surface, as he chose his lure, his approach, as he watched for an energetic trout to break the surface and burst upward, tail flapping and body arcing, toward breakfast.

But for this moment, the euphoria was part of the ritual, and he knew then and there that they would share this with Kyle, they would make a voodoo of his first rigging for the harvest. The three veterans would show him the ropes, pin bright-colored flies on his hat, and make sure he was properly suited up.

★ ★ ★

As they walked single file, the Judge leading the way and briefing Kyle about the river — "always respect it, be mindful of its current, take care on its slippery rocks" — Jeff found a certain reassurance in what was before him. The Judge, confident leader, followed by Kyle, the newcomer, who was struggling to stay aright in the wake of what was his Gear. The very act of walking appeared to be a challenge and the young man clattered like a tinker's wagon.

Then there was Sam, with a rod that was missing guides and an old creel that was latched with a length of shoelace — tied on by one of his daughters after her puppy had chewed the leather flap to bits.

In spite of the differences, Jeff was secure in a sort of idealistic belief that both men, veteran and tyro, would succeed: they would Catch Fish.

And so it was that the four men arrived on the bank of the river just as dawn broke.

CHAPTER SEVEN

ॐ

BAIT: Anything that attracts fish or shellfish by scent and/or flavor. This includes any device made of feathers, hair, fiber, wood, metal, glass, cork, leather, rubber, or plastic which uses scent and/or flavoring to attract fish or wildlife.
— *Washington State Department of Fish and Wildlife*

Jeff's gaze absently followed the fly as it floated toward him, then on past. He'd had no luck, not a single bite, all morning. As much as he'd fought it, his mind wandered, and, true to the scales of balance that represented his astrological sign, his thoughts were split between two: the problem of storing the antiques, and the mystery of Bill's murder.

His legs were numb with cold, and the muscles in his shoulders were tense. Yet in contrast, the warm rays of the sun, combined with the big breakfast he'd consumed, had lulled him into lethargy.

He glanced across the stream at Sam, who was stooped over, examining a catch. Its iridescence glittered pink and silver in Sam's dark brown hands. Sam appeared to be checking for the adipose fin — the presence of one meant that by state law the fish must be returned to its habitat. He obviously found none, because he untied the shoelace on his worn creel and placed the rainbowed beauty inside as if he were depositing a role of hundreds into a vault.

Unless Jeff had miscalculated, that made the score Sam-4 (with two keepers), Jeff-0. He wondered absently how the Judge and Kyle were faring. They'd decided to head up around the bend. Jeff grinned as he recalled the picture of the young man, laden with tackle boxes, waders, nets, and creel, struggling to keep up with the Judge's long-legged strides. Kyle should catch a doozy, Jeff thought. Beginner's luck was not a force to sneer at. That was, if all of Kyle's fancy new equipment hadn't jinxed him.

A noise startled Jeff from his thoughts. He turned just in time to catch a glimpse of an elk crashing through the woods, dodging trees and leaping over obstacles. He strained, intently watching the elk's progress until it disappeared from view. Mesmerized, he didn't make the connection that something probably had spooked the beast.

"Talbot," a voice said softly.

Jeff jumped, slipped, and damn near lost his footing altogether on the rocks.

Sheriff McIvers stood on the edge of the bank, leaning toward him.

"A scream would've been less jarring, Sheriff."

"Didn't want to scare the fish," she said, maintaining a quiet tone. "Not that it would've mattered." She nodded toward the current. "I don't know much about your kind of fishing, but I do know you're not supposed to drown your flies."

Jeff's mouth opened slightly, and his gaze followed the line from the tip of his rod to a point far behind him downstream. He turned and reeled it in, the glint of the wet filament winking in the bright sunlight.

"I came out here to talk to you about the fish."

"They aren't biting for me today." He grinned and added, "Even when I do it right."

"Not these fish. The ones at Bill's. Those in the aquarium."

"Oh? What about them?"

"Well, I found three different species of fish on the floor, two more in the tank you guys set up. At least I think so. Could be double that, though, if they're like so many other living things that God blessed with fancy-colored males and hard-working but dull females. Anyway, I called the number for that pet store in Seattle that Bill had receipts from, spoke with a fella who hooked me up with a guy who's an expert on exotic fish, birds, snakes. Calls himself Raven. He's —"

"Calls himself what?"

"You heard right. Raven. I said, 'Like the bird?' thinking he'd come up with it because of his work. Know what he said? Said, 'Nah, like Poe. Edgar Allan?' I guess he wanted it to sound darker than *just* the bird."

"Then why doesn't he call himself . . ." Jeff paused. "Well, the fish names I know wouldn't make very good nicknames: Trout. Salmon. How about Dolly Varden?" Jeff winked at the sheriff. "There's an image for you next time you talk to the guy."

"Thanks a lot. He's coming out here after he gets off work tonight. Told me to bag the dead ones and put them in the fridge. I'd already thought that far. He says he can identify all of them. It might not give a lead on

Bill's time of death, but it can't hurt."

"Why did you want to tell me all this?"

"I thought you might want to meet this character, since I need you to come by the bait shop anyway."

"Me? Why? I already told you everything I know." Jeff's powers of concentration were bad enough, in light of Bill's death and the accident with the antiques. He didn't need to be drawn into a murder investigation, too.

"It's not about the case. I'd like for you to take a look at some old fishing stuff from Bill's collection. Might be able to get you the job of selling it, if you're interested."

Now, that's more like it, Jeff thought. What was today? Friday. That meant a fish fry tonight — if anyone was doing better than he was — followed by a trip down the road to Coop's Tavern for a few drinks and an update on the local gossip. He supposed he could drive separately. "Sure, I'll be there."

"Around seven, then?"

He nodded, and the sheriff headed back through the woods.

Jeff made an earnest attempt at fishing after the sheriff left, but didn't land anything. He waded to shore, struggling against the current. After eating a lunch of bologna and cheddar with crackers, he stretched out on a grassy patch to catch a nap. He suspected that his run of bad luck would continue into the afternoon, and he knew that tonight would be even later than last night had been. He felt a little guilty as he drifted off, relying on the others to furnish supper. But not guilty enough to keep him awake.

Sam rousted Jeff around dusk and teased him mercilessly as they made their way back to the cabin.

"The way my luck was going, I figured I'd put my time to a better — and much needed — use." He lifted the lid on Sam's creel. "What are you complaining about? Looks like you caught some granddaddies."

"Won't do much good, if last night is any indication. Lord, did you see how that Kyle eats?"

Jeff grinned. "Have a heart, Sam. He's still growing."

Kyle and the Judge were already at the cabin, cleaning a mess of trout. Beginner's luck had lived up to its promise, and Kyle's enthusiasm was contagious. Even though Jeff preferred salmon, he wasn't about to let on. A first fishing trip was a sacred thing.

After Sam had cleaned his catch, the four men went inside. They worked together in the large kitchen, mixing up batters and setting pots and skillets of oil to heat on all the rangetop's burners.

Timing was everything, and they succeeded in putting their feast on the table hot, crisp, and in tandem: fillets, hush puppies, French fries. Jeff opened containers of cole slaw and broccoli salad he'd purchased at the grocery deli, and the four men gorged themselves on the feast. They finished off with a pot of coffee and Sheila's Better Than Sex Cake.

When they were ready to leave for Coop's Tavern, Jeff told the others about the sheriff's request and said he'd catch up after meeting with her.

He arrived at the bait shop early, found Sheriff McIvers sitting in a rocker on the front porch. The rocking chair made her appear even more vulnerable than she had when Jeff had first seen her. Secretly, he was glad that he'd be here when this Raven guy showed up. He wondered if this had crossed the sheriff's mind and prompted her to invite him along.

He'd no sooner said hello when the low rumble of a beefed-up engine came from down the driveway. The sheriff stood, and both she and Jeff watched as an older Chevy Suburban pulled in and parked horizontally, giving them a full view of its glossy black profile. The windows were so black that Jeff suspected they had been painted and not merely tinted. The vehicle sat dangerously close to the ground, and he wondered how its driver had gotten it out there without poking a hole in the oil pan.

"Good God," said the sheriff as her other guest made his way down the path. "The things they'll do nowadays to get attention."

"I, uh . . . is this normal?" Jeff didn't like to think he'd been leading a sheltered life since leaving the Bureau, but his inner reaction to the sight before him revealed just how out-of-touch he really was.

Raven — and he was more raven than man — was six-foot-five and had hunched shoulders that gave the impression of a winged creature. His hair was unnaturally black, long and slicked back with some sort of pomade or wax that gave it the iridescent shimmer of feathers in moonlight. Black bead eyes were diminished by a large hooked nose, and his skin was as pale as Dracula's. He wore a black oversized slicker that nearly dragged the ground, above black boots made heavy by chromed hardware, and around his neck was a dog collar with silver spikes and a long chrome chain that dangled as if the young man had just broken loose.

Jeff turned to the sheriff. "In case I forget to tell you, I had a great time tonight."

"Uh-huh. *Pretty Woman*, right?"

"Hey!" Jeff exclaimed a little too exuberantly. "You're the first person, other than my wife, who gets it."

"My idea of a date is me on the couch with Richard Gere and a bowl of popcorn."

"My wife's housebound," Jeff announced, surprising himself. He hadn't intended to reveal anything about Sheila, and in the course of twenty-four hours, he'd told two strangers about her.

"Sorry. Makes me realize I don't have that much to complain about, huh?"

"Everybody's got something."

She took off her cap for an instant, started to replace it, then, with another look at the approaching apparition, she rolled the cap and stuffed it into her back pocket.

Jeff figured she was attempting her own little shock effect.

It worked, evident by the brief yet unmistakably startled expression that fluttered across Raven's face.

He made an obvious nod to the sheriff's head, said simply and with a sincere tone, "Cool."

"Thanks. Cost me a bundle."

Slowly, the realization of what she meant

seemed to hit. The young man looked away for a moment, then met her gaze again, back in character. "I could put together a list of herbs that might help, if you're interested."

"Can't hurt, right?"

Raven smiled, told her he'd fax it to her when he returned to the pet shop.

Jeff felt as if he'd slipped into a scene from a science fiction film.

The sheriff made introductions, then led the two men inside where she retrieved the baggies of fish from the refrigerator.

Raven began spitting out statistics like ticker tape. "Hatchet fish." He tapped two baggies containing fish with reddish brown markings. "They're what I think of when I hear, 'a fish out of water.' They die pretty fast.

"These pacus would've been next to go. Nickname: vegetarian piranha. They'll last maybe five minutes out of the water. Ten, tops."

"Vegetarian piranha?" Jeff studied the silver and black fish that looked as if a steam roller had gone over them. "Sounds like an oxymoron."

"It does, doesn't it? They're related to piranhas, they look like piranhas, but they're herbivores instead of carnivores — that's how they got their nickname. I've seen them suicide leap from their tank, then flop around so vigorously that they break their backs." Raven looked up. "Owning them is like taking care of a baby."

He walked to the makeshift aquarium and pointed out a species of brightly colored fish. "These beauties are koi. Some call them Japanese goldfish."

"They're not like any goldfish I ever had," said the sheriff.

Jeff studied the vibrant white fish with orange splashes. He said, "I'd be happy if I could catch salmon that size."

"They grow to fit the size of their environment. They're the ultimate exotic, in my opinion. They live, like, forever, too."

The sheriff said, "Forever, as in . . . ?"

"A hundred years."

"Impressive," Jeff said. "But how long does it take them to die? *Out* of water, not from old age."

"They're a heartier fish, but if you need it in exact *minutes,* I'll have to do some research and give you a call."

"Just don't kill one, okay?" The sheriff threw in.

"You're kidding, right? They cost thousands. People don't seem to care, though. They like koi because they're so colorful. They can even be seen in a dirty tank.

131

"That's where the plecos come in." Raven pointed out the other species in the tank.

"Plecos?" Jeff followed.

"Plecostomus. The pet store crowd calls them plecos, consumers usually call them sucker fish because they suck out the algae and keep the tank clean. Get 'em mad, and they have a cool mohawk. When they're calm, though, you can't even tell it's there. They pretty much hang out on the bottom or work their way up the sides, sucking like little vacuum cleaners." Raven's lips moved as if he were a fish underwater.

The sheriff leaned in close to the glass. "So, the plecos survive longer out of the water?"

"Yes, Ma'am. The other day, a friend of mine removed his fish from their tank so he could clean it. An hour later, he was putting the castles back in the tank, when a pleco darted out of one. So, yeah, they'll last a while."

The sheriff said, "It's beyond me how you can put all these different fish in one tank."

Raven shrugged a shoulder. "Some people won't put koi with other fish. Others say there's an order to things when you put together a controlled community, just like there is in the wild. They also do better if they grow up together. Plus, the bigger the tank, the more you can get away with — you just have to know what you're doing.

"Think of it like a corporation," he continued. "If the piranhas are the biggest, they'll come in and stake out the corner offices. Next in size will take what they perceive to be the next best cubicles, and so on and so forth, until each species has claimed its own territory."

"Well," said the sheriff, "they *were* in a large tank, till it got destroyed."

Jeff gazed at the surviving fish through the side of the tank. "So, you're saying that if these bad boys were still alive when we arrived on the scene, then the murder could've happened at least an hour before we got here?"

"You got it." Raven looked around. "Wow. A murder right here in this room. Need me to put a spell on it or anything?"

"Uh, no thanks." The sheriff took the young man by the arm gently and guided him toward the front door. "This was an isolated case, I'm sure."

"Okay," he replied doubtfully. "But if you change your mind . . ." He handed her a black business card with silver metallic lettering, then vanished.

Jeff peeked at the card. It read:

Raven
Tarot Readings, Exorcisms, Exotic Aquatics
Summon via: 555-Black

He shook his head. "You've gotta love freedom of expression."

The sheriff studied the card. "I suppose listing 'herbal remedies' would've ruined the mystique." She closed the door, then gathered the baggies of fish and returned them to the refrigerator. That chore done, she motioned for Jeff to follow her to the back room.

Two large cartons, identical except that one was sealed and the other wasn't, stood side by side on Bill's chipped enamel kitchen table. "Collection" had been written on the end of each with a thick black marker. The sheriff showcased them as if she were one of Bob Barker's Beauties.

Jeff opened the flaps of the unsealed carton, set aside a manila folder that rested on top of the contents, and glanced inside. A layer of small boxes, all in pristine condition, were fitted inside like Lincoln Logs. Carefully, Jeff removed them.

Below the first was another layer of the little boxes. He surmised that the large corrugated container held another six or seven levels. He could tell as he removed each that it likely held what its packaging advertised: an antique lure. The patent dates ranged from the early 1800s to the 1950s. Pinpointing their ages would require a lot of work. Jeff let out a low whistle as he stacked the tiny boxes on the tabletop.

"I knew Bill had quite a collection," Jeff said as he examined the contents of the small boxes, "but these are really cream of the crop. The contents of this single carton should bring several thousand —" He stopped. The coincidence of all the lures Kyle had brought yesterday was a little unsettling. Jeff wondered if Kyle knew more than he was letting on.

"Did you sell any of these to him?"

"Maybe. He bought quite a few fishing collectibles from me over the years, but — how many more cartons are at the house?"

"Another dozen or so, I'd guess. I didn't open the rest, so I can't say for sure what's in them."

"I wonder why he'd have them stored like this. I mean, you can tell from his shop that he liked to display his collection."

"Maybe his wife boxed them up. She said she couldn't get this junk out of *her* house fast enough."

"She gave these to you?"

"Yep. And, like I said, there's lots more

where these came from."

"But why? I mean, why would she give them to you? Did you confiscate them?"

"Jeez, Talbot, is that how you questioned suspects when you were an agent? No wonder you had to find another line of work."

"I didn't *have* to leave. I just have a hard time understanding people who think that fishing antiques aren't worth anything."

"On the contrary. She's *counting* on them being worth something. She just doesn't appreciate why they should be."

Jeff remembered the manila folder. He opened it, skimmed the neatly typed printout inside. "His documentation is certainly detailed, although it looks like he was as bad as I am." Jeff pointed out the coded columns. "Had his own brand of shorthand."

"I noticed that, too." The sheriff studied the columns. "I went through this one, compared it to the inventory you're holding. Some of the items listed aren't in the box."

"Maybe he was still working on it, you know, an ongoing project. Or —"

"But the boxes were sealed when Tanya Rhodes gave them to me."

Jeff raised a brow. "That doesn't make

sense. Why would he seal them up if he wasn't through recording everything? Unless he simply miscalculated how much he could fit into one box."

"Then why wouldn't he just fix the list and print out a new one? Isn't that what's supposed to be so damned appealing about computers?"

Jeff smiled. "That's what they say." He looked for markings on the second box, which was sealed. "I see that you haven't cracked this one open yet."

"Nope. I thought it would be a good idea to have an antiques expert on hand. CYA, they always say. It means cover your —"

"I know what it means, Sheriff. I'm not *that* squeaky clean." Jeff's attention went back to the carton. "Did you have any trouble getting these from Mrs. Rhodes?"

"No, actually. Especially when I mentioned that you were here for your annual fishing trip. You must've made quite an impression on Bill's little bride last year. She jumped at the idea of having *you* find a buyer for Bill's collection.

"So," the sheriff continued, "I told her I'd be happy to help her out by showing you these, then you could decide whether you wanted to represent the sale of Bill's collection."

"How accomodating of you. What were you really thinking?"

"I'm being honest. I thought you might want first crack at it." She paused. "I also thought it might come in handy that you used to investigate antique thefts for the FBI."

Jeff studied the sheriff. "You think the lures — either the ones at his house, or those stolen a few years back, or both — have something to do with Bill's murder, don't you?"

"I have to think everything does, until it proves otherwise. It might seem like a strange approach to you, but I haven't investigated a whole lot of murders. I'd rather be safe than sorry."

"Or dead."

"Something like that." The sheriff looked at him and cocked a brow. "How would you like to pay a visit to the widow Rhodes? She also jumped at the idea of my bringing you over for a look-see at the rest of the stuff. I guess she figures she has a better chance convincing you to oversee the sale than I do."

"I'm in. When can we go?"

"If there's one thing I've learned from fighting death, it's that you don't procrastinate."

CHAPTER EIGHT

࿔

CHUMMING: Scattering feed or other materials to attract fish to a location.
— *Washington State Department of Fish and Wildlife*

Getting to Bill's house took about ten minutes by way of the county road that wound around the lake. To cut across by boat, as Bill often did, would have shaved it down to two.

Jeff usually didn't like riding with someone else behind the wheel, but Sheriff McIvers proved to be a hell of a driver, quickly spotting a doe that darted into the road. After she effortlessly maneuvered around the scrambling, wide-eyed creature, Jeff relaxed.

"So, Sheriff, how is it you know about pickers? Are you into antiques? A collector?"

"I had an uncle who was a picker of sorts." She looked Jeff up and down, and added, "Although not like you, by any stretch of the imagination."

"What do you collect?"

"Who said I did?"

He picked up on her defensiveness. "I'd be surprised if you didn't collect *something*. Most people do, even if they don't recognize it as such."

"Okay. I have a little collection, but it's not really an *antique* collection."

"Yeah? What is it?"

She ignored the question. "We're here."

He decided not to press the subject. As the sheriff drove down the driveway, Jeff thought about the last time he'd been in Bill's house. What had it been? Three, four years? He recalled how comfortable Bill's place was, with its rustic lodge decor, warm Mission oak furniture, soft Pendleton wool throws, and blazing fire in the massive rock fireplace. Everything needed to chase away the damp Northwest autumns was there, behind the large wooden door with its antique iron fittings that Jeff could now make out in the light of the headlamps.

As Jeff and the sheriff climbed up the limestone path surrounded by a thick carpet of pine needles, he thought about Bill's pride in capturing the mood and feel of his late wife's lumberjack ancestors.

So absorbed was he in the lingering image of the warm interior that, when the door swung open to reveal the changes obviously incorporated by the new Mrs. Rhodes, his breath caught and he was overtaken by a coughing fit.

"Mr. Talbot!" The woman who had opened the door reached out a manicured hand. "I didn't mean to startle you."

Tanya Rhodes stood in the open doorway, the bright light from within out-lining her curves through an ice blue chiffon dressing gown with matching blue collar and trim that resembled a feather boa. Jeff gazed past the young, voluptuous blonde who stood before him and stared, bewil-dered, at the stark white walls, cold glass, and chrome that dominated the house.

"Mr. Talbot, are you all right?"

"Yes, yes, I'm fine." Jeff scrambled for an explanation. "I half expected Bill to open the door. The realization that he's gone just hit me."

Tanya Rhodes took his arm and pulled him inside. "It's quite shocking, isn't it?"

He caught a whiff of gin. "Yes, it certainly is." He realized that the young widow had no idea they were talking about two different things. He recovered a bit and added, "I can't imagine how difficult it must be for *you*."

"Oh, you have no idea." She looped her arm through his and squeezed his bicep. He consciously refrained from pulling away, and tried to convince himself that the grieving widow's behavior was a result of nerves and shock. Still, he looked over his other shoulder in order to assure himself that the sheriff was still on board. The look he received told him unmistakably that he was on his own as far as the blonde vixen was concerned.

Tanya led him across the white marble floor, her heels tapping a staccato *click, click* atop its polished surface.

"Here, let me take your jacket." She pulled at his coat.

"I'm fine, really. We won't keep you very long." He cleared his throat. "Sheriff McIvers tells me you'd like to sell Bill's antiques."

"Yes, how sweet of her to fetch you over here so soon." Tanya flashed a quick, shallow smile at the sheriff. "I really have no use for all that old stuff, you see, and friends tell me that the faster I get rid of Bill's things, the easier it will be to move past his . . . well, you know."

"That could be true," Jeff said, "but I don't want you to feel rushed."

"It's all right, really." She picked up a bell from the sofa table and rang it lightly. Presently, a white-haired maid appeared, the delicate white apron of her uniform noticeably in contrast with her thick black tights and heavy black sweater. "May I offer you something to drink?" asked their hostess.

"On duty," said the sheriff. "Thanks just the same."

Tanya gave her a look. "Suit yourself. You're not on duty, Mr. Talbot." She smiled warmly. "What'll it be?"

"Nothing for me. Thanks."

She shrugged then, turned to her maid. "I'll have the usual."

Jeff detected an ever-so-slight arch of the maid's brow before she nodded to her employer and walked to a bar setup on a chrome-trimmed credenza of light blue enamel.

"Tanya, I have to advise against your usual."

This new voice came from a man who stepped into the living room from a long corridor. He placed a small leather case on the floor, then took a coat from a hall tree. "That sedative I prescribed yesterday is powerful."

"Not even one little drink, Doctor?"

The man shook his head, and Jeff surmised that he'd dealt with the woman before. "Not smart, but maybe you can get your friend here to carry you to bed. You put a drink on top of those pills, and I'm quite certain you won't be able to walk there."

Tanya squeezed Jeff's bicep again. "He's up to it, I'm sure." She smiled suggestively.

Jeff pulled free, stepped closer to the sheriff.

The doctor turned to Jeff and lowered his voice. "She must have been drinking before I got here. She'll be a real mess if she doesn't choose one or the other soon."

After the doctor let himself out, the sheriff said, "Mrs. Rhodes, if you'd like, Mr. Talbot here can take the other boxes of fishing gear with him. He'll be returning to Seattle in a few days, and —"

"No need to explain. The sooner I get rid of that old fishing junk, the better. Follow me."

Jeff and the sheriff followed Tanya through the kitchen, which had been remodeled to match the living room, and through a door that led to a carpeted staircase.

Once in the basement, they walked

through a large, open area with equipment that would have given any Bally fitness center a run for its money. Beyond the gym, Tanya opened a door and flipped on a switch. The large room was Jeff's first indication that he was, indeed, in Bill Rhodes's home.

The office was paneled in warm wood tones, and a good portion of the Mission oak furniture Jeff remembered had been crowded into this room. The walls were lined with old advertising signs, as well as shadow boxes and display cases full of lures and reels.

The only thing in the room that hinted of modernism was the putty colored computer. It stood cold and silent on an oak library table.

"All of Bill's stuff is there." She indicated several boxes stacked against the far wall.

"Did he tape them up?" the sheriff asked.

"I suppose so. At any rate, they were sealed when I first saw them."

"Mrs. Rhodes," Jeff said, "a box that the sheriff showed me earlier didn't have a complete inventory list. Do you mind if I take a look at Bill's computer files, see if he kept a folder with updates? It'll help me get the best price for you on his collection."

"Be my guest. Matter of fact, if you don't

find everything you need tonight, you can come back any old time for a visit." She shot a look at the sheriff and added, "you won't even need a police escort."

"Mrs. Rhodes?" The maid's voice interrupted from the top of the stairs. "Your lawyer just called, said there's nothing you can do about Mr. Rhodes's final wish."

Tanya's reaction — whether to the news, or to the maid's lack of discretion, Jeff couldn't be sure — was one of apparent anger. Her face reddened, her eyes narrowed, and her glamorous facade fell away like cracked plaster. The widow excused herself abruptly and went upstairs.

"I wonder what that was about," Jeff said after Tanya was out of earshot.

"About the funeral would be my guess. Bill left instructions that he is to be cremated and his ashes spread over the lake." McIvers grinned. "As you've no doubt guessed, Mrs. Rhodes despises everything to do with fishing. She's furious that there won't be a conventional service."

"Have the other arrangements been made? Time, place?"

"Two o'clock tomorrow, at the bait shop's dock."

"We'll be there. Most of us, anyway. I can't speak for Kyle, since he didn't know

Bill." Jeff pressed a button to boot up the computer. "By the way, sheriff, you're not giving me much help here tonight."

"I told you I don't know anything about computers."

"That's not what I'm talking about, and you know it."

The sheriff's green eyes sparked. "Well, despite the fact that the dear widow is mixing sedatives and alcohol, you probably don't have to worry about your virtue being compromised. From what I hear, she's all sizzle and no steak."

"What?"

"You know the type. Flirts like there's no tomorrow, then turns cold as a fish when it comes down to it. You'd think, though, she'd have enough respect for Bill's memory to act a little more decent so soon after his murder." The sheriff pulled up a chair beside Jeff. "That's all hearsay, though. That, and what I've seen when my path has crossed theirs around town."

"What about the things your deputy was saying yesterday?"

"He has a real problem with talking out of school. Thing is, all that stuff about Tanya that comes out of the beauty shop is true."

"The bit about Gunther the personal trainer appears to be," Jeff said, with a nod toward the workout equipment in the next room. He scrolled through the computer's list of folders. "She's got a lot of curves, though, for someone who has a reputation of working out. Plus, she doesn't strike me as the type who would pump iron and chance breaking a nail."

The sheriff shrugged, then leaned forward and studied the computer screen. "How do you know what you're looking for in there?"

"Well, this stuff looks more organized than my wife's computer, which is saying quite a bit. See this?" He double-clicked a folder titled "Go Fish" and an infrastructure of a dozen more folders appeared. He opened a couple, then said, "Each of these has pages of notes and documentation about his collections." He shuffled through drawers of the library table until he found an unopened box of disks. "I'll copy the files onto these, then work on matching them to the contents of the boxes after I get back home. That way," he added, "I don't have to sit here and fight off the distraught widow."

"Didn't look to me like you were doing much fighting."

"Better watch out, Sheriff. Someone might mistake you for being a female."

The hurt look on the sheriff's face told Jeff that she'd misunderstood.

He tried to explain. "I wasn't implying that you're not a woman. I'm sorry if it came out wrong. But to me, the word 'female' connotates rivalry, jealousy. You know, hell-bent on scratching each other's eyes out."

She nodded. Her expression relaxed somewhat. "How long will it take to make copies?"

"Only a minute or so. Then I'll haul these boxes up to the car, and we'll see if we can get out of here before Tanya Rhodes abducts me."

CHAPTER NINE

៛

HARVEST RULES: You may not harvest any part of another person's daily limit, except as provided for under disability license.
— *Washington State Department of Fish and Wildlife*

Coop's Tavern looked like a forty-unit storage building outlined in an odd combination of neon and Christmas bulbs. Jeff parked the woodie well beyond the empty rows in order to separate and, hopefully, protect it from the pickup and shotgun crowd.

After he'd transferred the boxes from the cruiser to the woodie, he'd told the sheriff good night and said he'd see her at Bill's funeral.

He was suddenly anxious to catch up with his friends, see if he could get back into the normal routine of the fishing weekend.

He spotted Kyle and the Judge in a booth at the back of the room and began working his way around the perimeter of the dance floor. Several couples were crowded onto the glossy parquet, dancing to Dwight Yoakam.

"Hey!" Sam yelled.

He turned in time to see Sam abandon a young woman in mid-step, and caught the glare that should have been directed at her defecting dance partner. Jeff shrugged apologetically.

"It's about damn time you got here. What took you so long?"

Jeff glanced at his watch. Actually, he was surprised that he'd managed to squeeze so many events into a span of only three hours. He ordered a beer at the bar, then followed Sam to the booth where the other two men waited. Jeff gave them a thumbnail sketch of his evening, starting with the strange encounter with Raven and ending with the behavior of Bill's widow and the boxes containing his collection.

When he was through, the Judge said, "See? I should've pressed for host privileges last night and confiscated all of Kyle's lures."

"Patience, Judge. These will be for sale soon enough."

"Sure. *After* you've gotten first pick."

"Must be why I'm called a picker. Truth is, I doubt I'll find much in there that I want. Several of them probably passed through my hands on their way to Bill. How about I give you first shot at them?"

"That's more like it."

Sinatra began singing "My Funny Valentine," and a collective groan came from the crowd.

"*Damn* it, Val." The bartender yelled, as if he were correcting a child for the umpteenth time. "Am I gonna have to take that off the jukebox and hide it from you?"

"Go screw yourself, Max Cooper." The woman sitting at the bar started to take a drink, studied the half inch of amber liquid in the bottom of her glass, then added, "but not before you get me another one of these."

The Judge, who'd swiveled to get a look at the woman, turned back and clasped a hand around his glass of Scotch. "I've seen that gal put away her share of drinks over the years, but as I recall, she's usually a fun drunk — you know, flirty, dancing with anyone she can drag onto the dance floor."

Jeff frowned. "You know her?"

"God, no. Know *of* her, though. Hell of a dancer. You remember — wait, you left a day early last year. Sam, you remember, don't you?"

"I missed last year, *remember?*" Sam's tone echoed his still-harbored irritation at missing out on that trip.

The Judge stared blankly for a moment, then shook his head as if to clear the cobwebs. "Hell, I *am* getting old. The years are running together. Anyway, Val, aka Vanessa Valentine, pulled Gordy onto the dance floor and snuggled up against him like bark on a tree."

Jeff's brows shot up. "You're kidding, right?" He thought he knew everything there was to know about his friend, but he'd never seen Gordon Easthope dance. Old-fashioned Gordy, who still called kissing "sparking," and who believed in properly courting a lady. Jeff stole another look at the woman and wondered just how far Gordy's virtue had been compromised.

"Funny, Gordy never mentioned it." Jeff grinned. "I know what *my* first call's going to be when I get home."

Sam stretched in order to get another look at the woman. "Her name explains it, I guess. She looks like one of those boxes we used to decorate and take to school on Valentine's Day."

Jeff leaned a little to the left in order to see

what Sam was talking about.

Vanessa Valentine was wearing a tight leopard print sweater, pink with black spots, secured with buttons that caught the light and glinted pink like tiny prisms. The sweater was strategically unbuttoned to reveal a bit of cleavage, and the sleeves were pushed up to three-quarter length, exposing a thick dusting of gold-pink freckles on both arms. A mass of brassy red curls, loosely pinned up at the back of the woman's head, brushed against her slender neck. She fumbled with a disposable lighter in a shade of pink that matched her nails, got the flint to catch on the third pass, then with hands slightly trembling, she put fire to a cigarette held tight between bright pink lips. Jeff noted that the woman's face was lined and hard, but he suspected she'd been a real looker in her day.

"I don't know." Jeff straightened himself in the booth and took a drink. "Gordy could've done a hell of a lot worse."

"In his nightmares, maybe." Sam started to take a hit off his beer, then started snickering and set the bottle back down.

The Judge grinned. "She looks like fun to me." He cleared his throat, then added seriously, "Of course, I'm heading down the campaign trail and the post-Clinton rule book for politics is to stay away from females who look like fun."

Jeff wondered absently whether the Judge would ever remarry. His wife of thirty years had died about the same time Jeff had left the FBI.

"Have a heart, guys," said Kyle. "She looks like she's lost her last friend or something."

"Kyle's right," Jeff said. "You never know what drives people to do what they do."

"Or act how they act."

"Or," Sam said, "dress like a bottle of Pepto Bismol."

A barmaid in tight black jeans and a top cut to reveal her midriff stopped on the fly and said, "You fellas need to drink faster. Bring you another round?"

"Sure," Jeff said. "And while you're at it, give Miss Valentine a cup of coffee from me."

"It'll only piss her off."

"Tell her I'll buy her another drink if she gets someone to drive her home. Otherwise, the offer of coffee stands."

The waitress left without further comment, and Sam said, "What'd you do that for?"

Jeff shrugged. "What can I say? People like our Miss Valentine over there are per-

155

fect targets for shrewd pickers such as myself."

"Target, my ass," Sam said. "You're too damned honest to take advantage of a drunk, let alone a drunk woman."

"True enough, but I think Kyle has a point. Right now she needs a friend, and in my line of work, a little bread on the water never hurts."

The waitress returned with the beers, and Jeff checked the bar. In front of the lady in pink was a substantial coffee mug. "Well, that's reassuring." He nodded toward the bar.

"Yeah, well, that's what you get for thinkin'." The waitress set the drinks down with a thud. "She said, 'I'll take half a cup of coffee and you can make the other half Kahlua.' "

"Doesn't matter to me, as long as she's got a ride."

"She's got a ride all right. She said to tell you she'll be ready in a minute."

The waitress was gone before Jeff could unclamp his jaw and spit out a protest.

His three comrades roared.

Jeff fumbled with the key, unwrapping satiny strands from the six-inch-long mauve tassel that Vanessa Valentine used as a key ring. It was an old skeleton key belonging to a charming cottage at the end of a tree-lined street in a small community about five miles down the road from the bar.

Once inside, Jeff groped for a light switch. He found an ancient push-button apparatus and punched it. The room was illuminated softly with light from a crystal-prismed chandelier.

The place glittered with perfume bottles, hundreds of them, displayed on everything from shelves to bookcases to windowsills. The initial effect was decadence, something that one either nailed or missed by a mile when showcasing such an overwhelming collection.

Jeff's inebriated charge had a real eye for design, a talent he hadn't expected. She had taken her cue from the dominant labels and liquids, and had filled the small room with shades of gold, garnet, and sable. It was like stepping inside a box of lavishly wrapped chocolates.

He was debating whether to deposit Miss Valentine on the couch or ask whether she would be able to make it to her bedroom on her own, when she broke free of his hold and stumbled toward the kitchen.

". . . need another drink," she slurred.

Jeff grabbed her arms and guided her

toward the nearest chair. "Only if it's coffee, Ma'am. And no more of those half-cup tricks."

She scowled up at him, but didn't protest.

He found the kitchen quick enough, and the makings for coffee even quicker. On the countertop, next to a Bunn coffeemaker (his personal favorite for sheer speed since it kept a reservoir of hot water at the ready) was a large silver tray that held a well-used electric grinder and several varieties of beans in sacks and canisters. From the looks of things, Vanessa Valentine liked coffee as much as he did. He opened a sack of Tully's brand hazelnut beans and put a handful in the grinder.

After he got the coffee going, he returned to the living room, only to find his charge draped over the chair's arm, snoring softly.

He couldn't very well leave her like this, he decided, or her neck would never be the same. He located a light switch in the small hallway and set about determining which room was her bedroom.

It didn't take long. Although there were two small bedrooms in the cottage, it was easy to tell which one Miss Valentine slept in.

The first one he came to wasn't it. This one looked more like a quilt shop, and although it had an elaborate antique iron bed, no one could have lain upon it. Suspended just inches above the bed was a quilting frame that held a work in progress. He recognized it as the Double Wedding Ring pattern.

Around the room, every conceivable surface held bolts of fabric, plump-cushioned sewing baskets, and stacks of neatly folded finished quilts. He found a few more styles he recognized — Cup and Saucer, Rose of Sharon, Log Cabin — among several that he wasn't familiar with. Ms. Valentine hadn't struck him as the seamstress type.

He flipped on the light in the second bedroom, and any question he might have had about her collecting things in honor of her name was answered. Vintage valentines were tucked into French memo boards, mirror frames, and bulging albums opened for display. All the perfume bottles in this room were heart-shaped.

A long-haired feline with a snowy coat lay curled up in the center of the bed. The furniture was Louis XV Revival in superb condition and bearing an ornately carved shell motif. It had a warm patina that was difficult to achieve with new pieces. The cat raised its head and squinted green eyes at him. From its pink collar, Jeff assumed it was female.

"Scoot over, girl," he said as the cat stretched lazily. He turned down the bed linens, then returned to the living room to fetch the lady of the house.

The coffee's aroma teased his senses, and he wondered whether or not it would be proper of him to have a cup before he left. He'd earned it, that was for damned sure.

The question was moot. As he walked into the living room, the lady of the house emerged from the kitchen, carrying a complete silver tea service. She smiled, then wobbled slightly, as if the simple gesture had thrown off her balance. Metallic *tings* reverberated as the set jostled. The woman steadied herself before Jeff could offer any assistance and placed the laden tray on a butler's table near the sofa. After pouring coffee (with only a slight amount of spillage) into two mugs, she handed one to Jeff and sat in a plump chair. The resident feline promptly curled up in her lap. "Forgive me for not using china cups and saucers, but I'm fully aware I'm in no condition to pull off *that* balancing act."

"I . . ." Jeff wasn't sure what to say. He'd seen people before who'd appeared to suddenly sober up, but it usually took more than a catnap. "Thank you, Miss Valentine."

"No, thank *you*. Although I'm more distraught than drunk, I was certainly in no shape to drive. I appreciate your taking the time to get me safely home, Mr. — ?"

"Talbot. You're welcome. But, please, call me Jeff."

"If you'll call me Val, instead of Miss Valentine."

"Val, then." He looked around the room. "It was worth it — bringing you home, I mean — just to see this magnificent collection."

"So, you know antiques?"

"It's my business, actually. I'm a picker."

"Oh? Do you come across many perfume or scent bottles? I'm always looking for something to add to my collection."

"Not too often, although I recently acquired some in a large group of things. I can't promise anything, but there might have been one or two large ones, like those." He pointed out a pair of identical containers prominently displayed on the mantel. "Weren't they used for shop windows?"

"Yes, they were." She sipped her coffee. "They're called factices, which, basically, is French for 'fake.' They don't really contain perfume, since they were used for store displays. I'd love to have a few more, *if* your prices are within reason, of course."

"I'll see what I can do, once I have an inventory." He'd wrapped the glassware that was in the two houses so quickly that he couldn't be sure exactly what he did have. "You said 'perfume or scent.' Are there two types, or do both terms apply to one?"

She smiled. "It's refreshing to find a man so genuinely interested. Scent bottles usually refer to those bought empty and filled either with a woman's specific blend or choice of fragrances. They are also called noncommercials. A commercial perfume bottle is as the name implies — sold commercially with packaging designed to go with the specific fragrance it holds."

"That's good to know."

"If I may be honest, I'm surprised you didn't know that."

Actually, he knew more than he was letting on, but he'd learned that you could pick up a lot of valuable information if you just let the other person talk. He didn't want her to know that though, so he said, "One of the curses of being a picker is that you tend to become a jack of all trades, master of none. I've come across a few perfume bottles, but I've never gotten into the specifics. Can you recommend some reference books about them?"

"Sure." She walked to a bookcase near

the hallway and chose two volumes. "These will get you started without breaking the bank."

Jeff jotted the titles and author's names in his notebook. "Do you ever sell any pieces, or discover that you have duplicates and weed some out?"

"I've never bought a duplicate. Thankfully, I have a photographic memory for what's in my collection. Although you can get some of the Avon collectibles for about twenty dollars, a rare bottle by someone like René Lalique costs sixty grand."

Jeff's brow raised.

Val nodded, then continued. "As for the rest, my mother would haunt me from her grave if I even considered selling."

"Did you inherit the collection from her? Is that the reason you keep it?"

She thought a moment. "That's how it got started. Now, every time I add a new piece, I feel like we went shopping together."

"Collecting does get in one's blood, doesn't it?"

"You collect, too?"

"Probably more than I should."

"It would be hard, I'd imagine, being a picker *and* a collector. How do you ever part with your treasures?"

"Depends on the collection. I collect cuff links, for instance, but only those I would actually wear. Mostly, though, I remind myself that I've got bills to pay." He smiled. "If that doesn't make you a mercenary, nothing will."

They fell silent. Jeff drank his coffee, suddenly aware that he wasn't sure what else to say to this stranger. Antiques brought many different kinds of people together, but it was rare for a conversation to move beyond that world.

The woman studied Jeff a moment before speaking. "The bartender said you're the one who found Bill Rhodes yesterday. Is that true?"

"Yes, it is."

"I can't imagine why anyone would want to murder him. He was the kindest man." She shivered, shook her head violently. "I heard it was a horrible death."

The image of Bill lying on the floor surfaced in Jeff's mind. "Did you know him?"

"Sure. We have a pretty close-knit community out here."

Jeff suspected as much. Likely everybody knew everybody, especially those who frequented Coop's Tavern. Just like those who went to church, or had kids in school, or were active in the community would know one another. There was probably even a select group who crossed the line by visiting the tavern every Saturday night, then showed up at church on Sunday morning to confess their sins. Most, though, would have stuck to one type of life or the other.

Val was silent for awhile before she spoke again. "Not too long ago, we were both at Coop's. It was pretty quiet, and Bill was trying to tell me how handy the Internet was for finding antiques. I don't know anything about computers and besides, I'd much prefer to spend my time poking around flea markets and antique malls. But Coop told him he could use the computer in the office to show me what he was talking about.

"Did you know," she continued, "there's an International Perfume Bottle Association?"

"I don't doubt it. There's at least one club or organization or association for just about every collectible out there."

"Funny, I'd collected for years and didn't know that, until Bill accessed their Web site for me. Anyway, he showed me how to buy antiques on . . . what did he call it? . . . it's a place where you bid . . ."

"ehammer? eBay?"

"eBay, that was it. I remember, because I

asked him what 'Bay' stood for. I mean, 'hammer' is easy. Auction, right? Anyway, we were going to look up perfume bottles, and he sort of backed into the process by first checking some lures he was bidding on. He said he usually bid by proxy, so that he wouldn't get carried away and pay a lot more than something was worth. After looking in on those, he went back to square one and did a search for old fishing gear — reels, lures, stuff like that. As he was showing me how to get details of each item, he brought up a screen with a lure to show me that each entry had a photo and a more detailed description.

"Well," she went on, "that day was the only time I'd ever seen Bill Rhodes lose his temper. Suddenly, he jumped up and said he had to get home to check on something. He left so fast, I wasn't sure what to think. When I went back out front and told Coop, he agreed that Bill had seemed upset. He said that he'd tried to ask him what was wrong, but Bill acted like he hadn't even heard him.

"After a little bit, Coop picked up the phone to make a call, paused a second, then asked me if the computer was still on-line. I told him I didn't know a damn thing about that high-tech stuff. He asked me to watch the bar while he went back to the office and signed off."

Jeff leaned forward. "How long ago was that?"

Her forehead creased. "Let's see. Two weeks, maybe. You could check the football schedule. I remember that it was the day before the Seahawks' big game with the Forty-Niners, because all of Coop's suppliers were making deliveries."

Jeff remembered seeing a game schedule taped inside the pay phone he had used at the grocery store. "Are you sure Bill didn't say anything? Anything at all, even if it didn't seem important at the time. It might mean something now."

"I'm sure. You knew Bill. He was a talker, always had something to say. That's why it stuck in my mind. I'd never seen him just leave like that without a word."

Jeff thought about this bit of information while he finished his coffee, cursed himself for not thinking to check Bill's Internet bookmarks while he had access to the man's computer. He cringed at the thought of having to face Tanya Rhodes again on her own turf, but he might have to, if it meant finding some clue about Bill's murder. "I understand there's to be a service tomorrow afternoon."

Val nodded, now more subdued. "His wife is furious about it, too, from what I gather. I'm sure her ears are burning more than usual."

"Does she have any friends around here?"

"I honestly don't know. But I do know this: She didn't treat Bill right. Anyone'll tell you that." She was fading, words trailing off. " 'Course, that's what he gets for jumping into marriage with someone he barely knew." She looked up, asked sincerely, "Are all men like that? So damned flattered by the attention that they don't even look past the silicone to see if there's a heart behind it?"

"No. That's why it's so noticeable when one of us does."

She stood and shuffled toward the door, effectively ending the conversation.

Jeff mulled over what Val had said about Bill's marriage, wondered whether there had been something between her and the victim before he had met and married Tanya. Jeff rose, followed the woman to the door.

She retrieved a light pink business card from a small sterling tray atop a table stained the color of rouge and handed it to Jeff. It put him in mind of the calling cards so popular during the Victorian era. "Please call me when you know about the perfume bottles."

"I will." He gazed at the card's font printed in garnet ink. Both of the capital *V*s in *Vanessa Valentine* appeared to be three-fourths of a stylized heart.

Jeff bid his hostess good night.

As he drove back to the cabin, he pondered an evening that had been full of intriguing women. Women who had all known the victim. . . .

CHAPTER TEN

ॐ

Piscator non solum piscatur
(There is more to fishing
than catching fish.)
— *Dame Juliana Berners*

"Well, well, look what the cat done drug in," Sam said around a mouthful of pancakes.

"He *is* the cat," said the Judge. "As in *Tom*cat."

Sam let out an exaggerated *meow*, then all three men at the table laughed.

"You could've woken me up." Jeff glared at them halfheartedly, then poured coffee into the biggest mug he could find. "That old alarm clock failed me this morning."

"Wasn't the clock that failed you," Sam said. "It went off, and you slapped at it a few times till it took pity on you and settled down."

"Tell you what," the Judge said, the corners of his lips twitching. "Tonight, why don't you share the women with those of us who don't have any waiting at home? That way you won't be so tired come tomorrow morning."

"I thought you were staying away from questionable women, Judge. Political image to keep, and all that."

"Oh, I don't know." The Judge winked at Sam, making sure Jeff could see the gesture. "It's pretty remote out here. I thought Kyle and I might take Miz Valentine and the Widow Rhodes out dancing this evening. Unless you have dibs on both of them again tonight."

"What can I say? I'm damned irresistible."

"If you have to say it," Sam announced, "then you ain't."

Jeff ignored the comment and went to the stove where he filled a platter with flapjacks, scrambled eggs, sausage links, and fried potatoes.

He got to the table as the others finished eating.

Sam started clearing the dishes. "Didn't I hear last night that Bill's funeral is this afternoon?"

"Two o'clock." Jeff gulped coffee.

"Should we meet back here at, say, twelve-thirty? That'll give us time to get cleaned up and eat lunch. We can ride over together."

"Sounds good." The Judge's tone left the impression that the vote was unanimous.

Jeff was having another nonproductive day on the water, despite his efforts to concentrate on his form. It was as if the fish sensed his tiredness, his various irritations, his lack of concentration. He was preoccupied with everything from the truck accident to all the work he had waiting for him back in Seattle to — and he'd fought this one — the mysterious murder of Bill Rhodes. Hell, he had to admit it, he'd consciously tried to squelch his investigative instincts. He hadn't been asked to help, hadn't really even been asked his opinion. The sheriff had included him in last night's visit to Tanya Rhodes because of Bill's collection — nothing more, nothing less. But something about it bothered him, and as he worried a knot in his fishing line free, he tried to do the same with the tangle in his brain.

He went over the events of the last thirty-six hours. At first, he'd thought Tanya's blatant flirting was what didn't sit well, but after deeper consideration, he realized that

that wasn't it. He didn't approve of her actions, but he believed they could be chalked up to a Molotov cocktail of booze and pills poured over raw nerves and lingering shock.

He tied on a dry fly and false cast a few times, the metronomic movements setting his mind into a rhythm that helped unwind his jumble of thoughts.

He went over his conversations with the sheriff, Tanya Rhodes, even Raven and the three men he shared a cabin with. He thought about the beauty shop gossip that the sheriff's deputy, Roy Manning, had shared. It, combined with his look at the remodeled interior of the Rhodes's home, gave a picture of someone who could go through money easily: shopping, golf courses, personal trainers. It took a moment before something else came to him. Then, suddenly, it was there twice.

Real estate. "Roy-Boy" had mentioned it, then the sheriff had said something about a real estate agent waiting for Bill's lunch break. Likely, Bill's refusal to talk to the agent was the catalyst for Tanya's anger.

This new realization bothered Jeff, but he wasn't sure whether it was because the real estate angle shed suspicion on the new widow, or because his own instincts weren't as sharp as they used to be. What about the sheriff's instincts? Shouldn't she have put those two things together?

He reeled in his line while he thought about his conversation with Val and the information she'd given him that Bill had been upset over something on the Internet. He should've done more digging into Bill's computer when he'd had access to it the night before. All told, however, his experience on-line wouldn't fill the toes of his waders. He made a mental note to give Sheila a call for a refresher course. She, like several million others, was hooked on the World Wide Web. And, as strange as it seemed to those who were hooked, many people in the antiques business weren't.

Jeff was one of *them*. Internet surfing wasn't something that naturally came to his mind when he considered recreational pastimes. And because of that, he'd have to return to the Rhodes house. Tanya's house.

That would instigate some major rib-jabbing from his comrades. But he had no choice. He knew he'd get a lot more cooperation from Tanya Rhodes than the sheriff would. The woman hadn't even questioned his request to check the computer files but had, in fact, encouraged him to come back.

You go with your strengths, Jeff thought, and his strength in this case was simply that he was a man. And while Tanya was busy flirting, her guard would be down. He would need to be sharper than he'd been the night before, be more prepared, and not allow himself to be flustered by her advances.

Thank God I have an understanding wife, he thought.

As he leaned to cast again, he saw the sheriff walking along the bank toward him.

"You might as well take up fishing, Sheriff." Jeff made his cast, then turned back to the bank. "You're making a regular habit of visiting my secret fishing hole."

She waded out, seemingly oblivious to the fact that she wasn't wearing waders. She lifted the lid of the creel on his hip, peered inside. "Yeah, it's so secret, the fish don't even know about it. You'd have better luck if you set the creel down, propped open the lid, and waited for a fish to jump in, kamikaze fashion."

"I won't deny that. My spirit wants a relaxing morning on the river, but my mind keeps wandering to things like accidents and murder."

"You and me both. Murder, anyway." She paused. "Listen, you said you had two other friends coming out here. Did they show up?"

"Sure. Well, one's a new guy that the Judge invited for the first time this year. But, yeah, they both made it in Thursday. Why?"

"Just trying to establish when everyone arrived. Do you know what time they got here?"

"No, but I can ask Sam. He said Kyle was already at the cabin when he pulled up."

"Sam's the one you know."

Jeff nodded. "Sam Carver. Known him for years."

"Which one is the attorney?"

"That would be Kyle Meredith."

The sheriff jotted the names on a notepad. "So, Kyle Meredith, who was supposed to be giving a deposition Thursday afternoon, arrived early."

Another thing I didn't think of. Jeff kept his face expressionless. "Listen, I can try to narrow down the times of arrival if you want me to. Kyle might be less wary talking to me instead of you."

"You've got a point."

"Did you learn anything else about the real estate angle?"

"Rumor, mostly. Some of Coop's regulars are saying that Tanya was putting the squeeze on Bill to sell the bait shop."

"I can't see that happening."

"Neither could he, apparently. It gets better, though. Turns out, Bill's truck wouldn't start after lunch, so the real estate guy gave him a lift back to the shop."

"Uh-huh. Anyone see Bill alive after the Good Samaritan left?"

"Now, that would depend on whether or not the Good Samaritan killed him, wouldn't it?"

"What does he say?"

"Says he didn't do it, of course. Does admit to taking advantage of having Bill as a captive audience, though. He's a high-pressure bastard, I can attest to that. Maybe my detective or the M.E. will turn up some tangible evidence soon, so I can stop playing twenty questions with no answers. In the meantime, I'm checking his alibis."

The sheriff leaned around Jeff, looked to where the fishing line had drifted. "Hey! I think you just snagged one!"

Instinctively, Jeff raised the rod and pulled slightly on the line. "I'll be damned." He wondered who was more surprised, he or the fish.

"Shouldn't you be reeling him in? Come on, don't lose him!" In one swift move, the sheriff jerked the cap from her head, shoved the notepad inside, and crammed the cap back on.

She then grabbed hold of the pole with Jeff, and he thought how he hadn't seen this much excitement over a fish since Sam was sixteen and landed a thirty-pound tarpon.

Jeff relinquished the rod and reel.

"Okay, turn the reel a couple of revolutions."

Before she could, he heard the high-pitched buzz of the line feeding out. "He's smokin'! Can you feel him moving? Okay, start reeling, slow and steady. There you go. Now pull him some, then reel in your slack."

The sheriff held on, followed Jeff's instruction, brought the catch steadily closer.

"Okay," he said, "reel in more slack. There! You've got the hang of it. Now, bring him on in."

Jeff couldn't have been prouder. The sheriff made it look like she'd been angling for years. She was a natural. He locked the reel when she'd finished, then squatted and took hold of the catch. "You've got a beauty here, Sheriff. Twelve, maybe fourteen pounds. One of the finest steelheads I've seen. Just look at him shine like a silver platter."

"Not me. You caught him."

"The hell I did. He would've nibbled and moved on if you hadn't been paying attention." Jeff removed the hook from the fish's lip then hoisted it by the gill. It wriggled, flipping its tail and sending an arc of water through the air.

"Here," Jeff said. "Take hold of him by the gill like this, and he won't be able to get you with a fin."

The sheriff took the glistening silver creature, then whooped like a warrior. "Now I get it. I see why you guys do this. Damn you, Talbot, you've got me hooked."

Jeff couldn't wipe the grin off his face. There was no pleasure quite like that of a person's first catch. "You should have it mounted, put it over your mantle or in your office. Take it to that taxidermist at the edge of town — what's his name?"

"Tommy?"

"Yeah. Take it down there, my treat."

The sheriff started to protest.

"Don't argue." He smiled. "Let me do this."

She paused a moment, then gave him a decisive nod. "Help me find something to put him in."

They walked back to the cabin, where Jeff rummaged around and found an old plastic bait bucket with a lid. He half-filled it with water, secured the trout inside, and told the sheriff to get down to Tommy's before he closed for Bill's memorial service.

After the sheriff drove off, Jeff sat on the

179

steps of the porch and waited for his three fishing buddies to return. He was still sitting there grinning when they walked up half an hour later.

"Why, you sly ol' dog," Sam said. "You finally caught one, didn't you?" He stepped up on the porch, followed by Kyle and the Judge.

"Sure did."

Sam opened the creel. "Well, where the hell is it? Wasn't it a keeper?"

The Judge stepped closer to take a look. "Rotten as his luck's been, we should've told him to take a damned picture."

"The sheriff has it."

Kyle's eyes grew wide. "The sheriff *confiscated* your fish?"

"What? Oh, hell. No, she didn't confiscate my fish." Jeff stood. "You see, it was like this. I didn't know —"

"Buddy," Sam said, "you can stop right here. That's already the damnedest fish story I ever did hear."

"If you don't believe me, go ask her. Matter of fact, you can ask her at Bill's funeral."

Sam shook his head pitifully. "If you can't do any better than that, I'm giving you canned tuna for lunch."

Sam, Kyle, and the Judge went inside, leaving a speechless Jeff behind.

CHAPTER ELEVEN

જ્જૈ

Be Quiet, and go a-angling.
— Izaak Walton
The Compleat Angler,
1653–1655

Black bunting sagged over the bait shop sign, concealing the business's name. All that remained visible were the words: BILL RHODES, PROPRIETOR.

Jeff made the left turn off the highway and pulled in behind a long line of vehicles.

"Quite a turnout," said the Judge.

"Yeah," Sam said, "I'm glad it's not raining. Bill would've wanted to be on the river on a day like today."

Jeff couldn't argue with that kind of thinking. Indian summer had given Bill a fine one for his final castoff. "Looks like this is going to take awhile." He turned to the

Judge, who was riding shotgun. "Okay if I use your cellphone?"

"Sure. It might actually work now. Sometimes I think they scramble the signals at night, because that's when I'm supposed to have the most free minutes."

"Wouldn't put it past them." Jeff punched his home number and hit Send.

"Sheila?"

"Well, this is a surprise. Everything okay?"

"Sure, we're doing fine."

"What happened? Did you tear into my Better Than Sex Cake and decide to let me know that it is?"

"Not a chance." Jeff's face felt hot. He didn't want to talk about their personal life while he was in a car with three men.

"I see. You're not alone, are you?"

"That's right."

"Okay, I'll behave. You must be calling for something specific then."

"Yeah. We're at Bill's service, waiting to park, so I thought I'd get some computer advice I'm going to need later." As Jeff took a notepad and pen from his glove compartment, he explained his need to forward Bill's favorites list to her computer. The Judge held the pad steady while Jeff jotted a shorthand version of her instructions.

"Kyle," the Judge said over his shoulder, "you'd better watch him. He's about to make off with your half of our double date."

Jeff said good-bye, then cut the connection. "Nah, I'd rather go to Coop's after this, toast Bill a time or two." He eased the woodie into a vacant spot. "I'll see if I can catch Tanya tomorrow before I leave."

"Sounds like a plan," said Sam as they crawled out of the car.

They walked past the bait shop toward the grassy slope that led down to the waterfront, and Jeff noted with relief that someone had thought to remove the yellow tape from around the building. He shivered slightly as he remembered finding Bill on the floor less than forty-eight hours earlier.

The uncovered dock was primitive but sturdy, and large enough for five or six vessels to tie onto. The *Rhodes Torpedo*, Bill's vintage Chris-Craft, was docked there alone, empty.

Jeff remembered Bill's excitement at taking ownership of the 1941 mahogany runabout. He'd named it the *Rhodes Torpedo* for two reasons: most obvious was the coincidence that he shared his name with the Shakespeare Company lure. A bonus came when Bill discovered that the lures with that name that he'd inherited from his father weren't those produced in the mid-1930s, as he'd originally thought, but rather those of the same name made a quarter century earlier. He'd sold them in order to buy the boat. That's when he'd begun to collect and study lures in earnest.

Jeff and the others positioned themselves near the back of the group as the clergyman began the service.

Jeff looked around, curious whether or not he knew many of the attendees.

He spotted Tanya Rhodes and the doctor he had seen at the Rhodes house the night before standing at the front of the crowd. They were gathered with a handful of others in a half circle near the land's end of the dock.

Standing beside Jeff, like so many Back-Row Baptists, was a group of men in blue jeans and dark blue bowling shirts emblazoned with Bill's shop's logo. In front of the bowlers was the Rhodes's maid, along with several of Coop's regulars, and Coop himself standing beside Vanessa Valentine. Val wore a pink suit and carried a pink handkerchief that fluttered in her hand when she dabbed daintily at her eyes.

A group of waitresses — Jeff recognized them as employees from Ruby's Diner by their uniforms of red dresses with starched white collars — formed a row across the center of the crowd as if they were a stripe on the flag. They would have just finished up from lunch shifts, he supposed, and hurried out to pay their respects.

He spied Sheriff Colleen McIvers, in uniform and cap, and at that instant she turned. Their eyes met, they exchanged a quick, knowing grin, and Jeff suddenly didn't give a damn whether or not his buddies believed him about the morning's catch.

Bill Rhodes would have wanted it this way, wanted people to come as they were, to smile and appreciate the meaningful little things, and in whatever small way be drawn closer to one another as a result of his passing.

After the pastor finished his remarks, he introduced a man as Bill Rhodes's brother, Jim. The man, although obviously younger by several years, bore a remarkable resemblance to the deceased. He wore a well-tailored black suit and tie, and Jeff guessed by his apparent comfort in the dress clothes that he was in the type of work that dictated similar attire on a daily basis.

Jeff would have been dressed much the same way for such a somber occasion but, of course, he hadn't known that a funeral would be part of the fishing weekend. He was thankful, at least, to have had a tweed sport coat with him from Thursday's work morning.

Mr. Rhodes began. "Thank you for joining us today. Your presence shows that Bill was well regarded and, I assure you, that will help us as we try to adjust to life without him."

He paused and smiled. "Bill and I fished every river and pond and stream within walking distance of this very spot while we were growing up, and it's always prompted warm memories when I've made visits — albeit infrequent — back to this part of our great country.

"I left here with far too much exuberance, and worked many sixty-hour weeks in pursuit of what I thought was the good life. I now realize that Bill was the wise one, the one who did what he loved and held fast to nature's soul."

The man clutched his fist to his mouth for a moment, then cleared his throat and opened a slim, bright-colored volume, which had been secured under his arm.

"I'll share with you a poem that captures Bill's devotion and reverence for the outdoors, and for the life he chose. It's what I believe he might have said had he been given to the written word.

"So, please, think of Bill as I read 'Romancing the River,' by Laurie Wagner Buyer.

Until I have felt underfoot her every curve
and bend
and heard the sound of her rippled voice
changing from chute to riffle to pool where
willows
drape reflections of her thousand faces,
how can I say I know her?

Until I have whispered to her in wonder,
stretched
out open on her soft and grassy sides or
reached shyly
into the unknown clefts of her undercut banks
and delved the old mysteries of her wild run-
ning,
how can I say I want her?

Until I have met and mastered the minds
of other worshippers — occult osprey, reclu-
sive brown,
flash fire of leaping rainbow and hidden
heron who
rises from the water phoenix-like, a cloud of
mystic smoke —
how can I say I accept her?

*Until I have walked alongside her in every
   waking
hour, dawn through dusk, and longer still,
   night into day,
and seen her dark flanks caressed by sun, sil-
   vered with
starlight and drank mesmerized from her
   secret springs,
how can I say I understand her?*

*Until I have held the haunting silence of her
   winter
heart in my shaking hands, counted the
   quick pulsed
flood of spring awakening, yearned for the
   ripe beauty
of her summer dress and coveted her autumn
   glory,
how can I say I possess her?*

*An hour or two is never enough. Even of-
   fering
one day diminishes the devotion she so de-
   serves.
Until I plunge into giving everything, vulnerable,
as naked and unashamed as her own soul,
how can I say I love her?"*

When he'd finished reading, Jim Rhodes

passed the book to the pastor, then took off his suit coat and handed that to him as well. While everyone waited silently, he climbed into the waiting boat, rowed to the center of the lake, and scattered Bill's ashes onto the water's calm surface.

Jeff brushed at a tear with his knuckle, but he couldn't be sure whether it was a result of the touching scene before him, or the fact that, try as he might, he couldn't recall his last conversation with the man who was now and forever gone.

It seemed hours before anyone moved, and those who did, did so hesitantly. Then, people funneled into a single row toward Mrs. Rhodes, and Jeff's foursome followed suit.

Tanya wasn't dressed in typical widow's weeds but rather wore a tight-fitting black suit of a fabric that reminded Jeff of the shiny sharkskin suits from the fifties. He noticed that occasionally her calf muscles gave way for an instant, at which time her spiked, black patent heels sank into the ground.

Jeff overheard the widow's comments to different people as they filed through to pay their respects. Statements such as, "This was Bill's idea, you know," and, "I do apologize for having to *drag* everyone out here like this," and, to some, "Come to the house after, okay?"

Jeff placed her in a category of people who resented being put in a position that they thought was orchestrated for the sole purpose of bringing embarrassment to *them.*

He stayed back, allowed his three companions to fall into line in front of him. The sun disappeared suddenly, and the wind picked up, blowing a chill from across the water. He was glad it had held through most of the service.

Tanya's irate voice got his — and everyone else's — attention. "It's bad enough that you would show your face here today, but couldn't you have at least had the decency to wear black?"

Jeff leaned over in time to see Vanessa Valentine draw herself up. Even from this distance, he detected her struggle for composure. Her suit was fashioned of fuschia linen, with a peplum jacket that accentuated her tiny waist.

"That shows how much you know. Bill despised black at funerals." Val raised her chin. "Besides, this was his favorite outfit on me . . . in public, that is."

Val turned and walked away, maintaining her composure as she climbed the hill toward the parking lot.

Jeff's three friends turned in tandem and

raised their brows. When it came their turn to greet the widow, they did so solemnly, yet quickly. Then they walked to where the sheriff stood alone by the dock, and Jeff wondered offhandedly whether they would try to confirm his fish story.

He was the last of the mourners in line, and Tanya took his hand in both of hers. "You *will* come by the house this evening, won't you, Mr. Talbot?"

"Actually, I should leave that time for you and your family. But, if I may, I'll stop by tomorrow before I head back to Seattle. Say, one o'clock?"

"That's even better," she said. "We'll have more time alone."

Something in Jeff told him to go along with her for now. The woman aroused nothing more in him than his curiosity, and he hoped that if he befriended her, he might learn more about the scene that had just happened between her and Val. He forced a smile. "I'll look forward to it, then."

As he started walking away, a man he hadn't noticed before approached Tanya. This new man's attempt at keeping his voice down only added to the sense of urgency. "You really should get the ball rolling, Tanya, before that brother of his gives you any trouble."

Jeff's investigative instincts kicked in. He stalled, feigned dropping something in order to hear the woman's response.

"You worry too much, Mike." Her voice took on a hard edge. "Bill may have gotten the 'burial' he wanted — if you can call it that — but I made sure everything else was in my control."

"Just don't let anyone strong-arm you. Remember, you're totally within your legal rights to go ahead as planned."

"You think I don't know that?"

"Just keep your senses intact, okay?"

Jeff glanced over his shoulder. The man was taking quick strides up the hill toward the parking lot. Tanya had turned and headed toward a small group that included Jim Rhodes.

Jeff caught up with his cohorts.

"What did you think of that little outburst?" the Judge asked. "It seems that my date for tonight was dallying with the deceased."

"You're kidding," said the sheriff. "You've got a date with Val?"

"Not really, Sheriff. Just a little fishing cabin humor."

"That — the cat fight I mean — isn't all that's fishy," Jeff said. He nodded toward the hill. "Sheriff, who's the skinny, bald guy making a beeline for the parking lot?"

She turned to get a look. "That's Michael Pratt, hotshot real estate agent. Why?"

"I just overheard him talking to the new widow. They've got something on the front burner, I can guarantee you that."

"I'm not surprised. Did I tell you he's the one who dropped Bill off at work Friday after lunch? I'd best pay him a little visit." She started to walk away, then turned. "See you fellas later at Coop's?"

"Wouldn't miss it," Jeff said.

CHAPTER TWELVE

❧

Washington State Law requires return of
your catch record . . . *even if nothing is
caught.*
> — *Washington State Department
> of Fish and Wildlife*

Jeff pulled into the parking lot at Coop's
Tavern and, in spite of the downpour that
had started when they'd left the bait shop,
parked in a space even farther away than the
night before.

"Damn, Talbot." Sam crawled out of
the backseat and gave the door a push.
"She'd be hard enough to find if we spent
all night drinking Shirley Temples. We
don't have a popsicle's chance in Tijuana
of locating her after a few hours of
drinking each other under the table. And
it's raining, to boot. The least you

could've done was let us off at the door."

The Judge pulled his mackinaw tighter. "I don't know, Sam. The brisk walk back out here will likely sober us up come ten or eleven o'clock."

"Ten o'clock?" Kyle said. Jeff could see the whites of the young man's wide eyes. Then Kyle grinned. "I guess it's true what they say. I'll have to see if the jukebox has 'Too Old to Cut the Mustard' on it. I'll play it in your honor, Your Honor."

"You'll be singing a different tune," Jeff said, "after the Honorable Judge Richard Larrabee rousts you out again at four-thirty tomorrow morning." Jeff swung open the door to the bar, and the four filed into a motley mix of everything from plaid flannel to sequins.

They headed for an empty booth, surprised that it *was* empty until a drop of water splashed into a waiting puddle in the table's center. Sam grabbed an abandoned rag off a corner of the bar and primly placed it down the length of pine as if it were a fancy table runner.

The waitress came by and took their orders, leaving behind a wooden bowl filled with party mix. Jeff grabbed a handful, then leaned back and looked around.

There were several knots of people in the

place. He spotted many that he'd just seen at Bill's memorial service, gathered in groups throughout the bar, nodding and smiling in that poignant way that told him they were reminiscing over the deceased, and toasting his memory with the first of many glasses. Underneath most of the expressions lay the unmistakeable gratitude that it hadn't been them who'd had a run-in with a murderer. The more they drank, Jeff knew, the more boisterous the place would get, the more fantastical the fish stories. It was the best send-off they could give to a man like Bill Rhodes.

The waitress returned with their drinks. "Where's your girlfriend?" she said with a sly glance in Jeff's direction.

"I thought you might be able to tell me."

"Haven't seen her today. Which isn't like her, I might add."

Jeff shrugged, and the barmaid did the same.

After she walked away, Kyle said, "Do you think Miss Valentine's okay?"

"Sure," Sam said. "She's probably just laying low after that little run-in with the wife, you know what I'm sayin'?"

"Thing is," Jeff said, "that run-in probably added her to the sheriff's suspect list. And, if I were the sheriff, I'd add Tanya

196

Rhodes and that real estate agent to it, as well.

"We may not see the sheriff, either," he continued, "depending on how many alibis she's been able to track down. Have you ever seen a town more like Peyton Place than this one?"

"Not in a hell of a long time," the Judge said. "Give me the big city any day."

"Hell, Judge, if you feel that way, you might as well head over to that other Washington."

"No, thanks."

"Hey," Kyle said, "there comes the sheriff now. Judge, here's your chance. You could always take *her* on a date if Miss Valentine doesn't show."

The Judge looked doubtful. "She's not really my type. Then, there's the conflict-of-interest issue to consider. And —"

"There's my fishing buddy!" The sheriff pointed at Jeff, then waved her hand as if she were directing traffic at a four-way. "Get out here and help me celebrate my first catch. I haven't been on a dance floor in a hundred years."

"*And,*" the Judge continued with an obvious rewriting of his interrupted speech, "Talbot, here, seems to have already gotten that vote."

As Jeff's three friends looked at one another and snickered, Jeff caught a lightning-quick flash of something else in Colleen McIver's gaze.

"I thought you'd never ask, Miz McIvers." He pushed his way out of the booth amid jabs and inuendos, then said, "You fellas see if you can behave yourselves."

Although Jeff was a good dancer, he'd never actually tackled the country western steps that were so popular at Coop's. The tavern had to be the only place within a thousand miles of Seattle that played that kind of music. The sheriff was a natural, though, and led him into a two-step rhythm to some twangy lyrics he wasn't familiar with. He concentrated on getting the dance steps down before he tried to carry on a conversation.

"You know, Sheriff —" he watched his feet as he spoke — "one of the biggest things I miss about working in law enforcement is that unspoken knowledge, that connection, that our particular level of officers has. I realize I'm no longer an officer, but some things always stay with you. It's interesting, isn't it? Those who are on the courtroom level never seem to catch our signals."

"Yep, comes in handy, don't you think?"

"Very. Now, what have you got?"

"A pretty fair list of suspects, as you know, with more alibis than George W. has cowboy hats. That, in and of itself, isn't surprising. But, the thing that *is?* They're checking out, one right after the other."

"What does your detective say about it?"

"Same thing. I've done the initial contacts, he's done follow-up. Everything that's looked promising has hit the wall like a crash-test dummy. Matter of fact, you can skip questioning Kyle Meredith. His deposition was rescheduled right after the Judge left the courthouse. He went to his apartment to load his car — landlord supports his story."

"That took some strategy. His car's no bigger than your pocket."

"Regardless, I've confirmed travel times. He wasn't here," she said. "That brings us to Mike Pratt, the real estate agent. He'd gone into Seattle on Thursday, right after he'd dropped Bill off at the bait shop. *That* raised a flag, let me tell you. But a check into his routine confirmed that he's made the same trip the third Thursday of every month for two years."

"That could be a cover, though. Perfect time to pull something, right before you're headed out of town."

"I thought of that. But he gave me another alibi, too. Said he saw a beat-up old pickup with wildlife decals all over it pulling in as he was leaving."

"Wildlife decals? Sounds like a too-many martini lunch, if you ask me."

"Nope. That's one of those things you don't see in fiction, because fiction's supposed to make sense.

"Retha Dobbs," she went on. "That's the woman who drives the pickup he saw. She's about the nearest thing to a hermit we have around here. Loves hunting and fishing, keeps that old International pickup held together with twine and threats, and it runs like a Timex. She'd shop at Bill's for things like milk, eggs, toilet paper, even though it was more expensive just so she wouldn't have to deal with the people in town.

"I found her a half hour ago, cleaning her rifle for deer season. She'd talked to Bill around one-thirty Thursday afternoon. Said Mike was pulling out when she got there, and that it was a good thing. She was tired of him harassing her to sell her lake-front property."

The next tune started. Jeff was getting the hang of this two-step business and didn't have to look at his feet anymore. "Have you heard back from that Raven character yet?"

"No, come to think of it. I'll give him a call."

Jeff thought back to the scene at the funeral. "Maybe there's something to Tanya Rhodes's insinuation regarding Val."

"Yeah, well, jealousy cuts both ways."

"Listen," he said, "I've got to go back out to Tanya's tomorrow, and, much as I dread putting up with her flirting, I could play along and try to find out why an old affair was still bothering her."

"It's no secret that Bill and Val had something going."

"Yeah, but why would Tanya have brought that up? I mean, it looks like she was the winner. Why would she care about Bill's past affairs?"

The sheriff shook her head. "You really are naive, aren't you?"

Jeff was surprised. "I thought —"

"All you guys think that if you've got a bombshell at home, then everything's picture perfect. Didn't you learn anything from Frank Gifford?

"Sure, Bill and Val were an item. For quite a while, actually. It was known from the get-go, however, that he didn't look at Val as marriage material. When he got blindsided by the nubile Tanya Price — she came for a price, all right — he dropped Val like a stone. He wised up pretty quickly, though, realized that his arm candy wasn't much for real conversation. Val got over being mad at him, and they drifted back into the same relationship they'd had before."

Jeff thought about this new information as the song faded. To his thinking, this actually made Val less of a suspect. If she'd recovered from her initial distress of being dumped and had resumed her relationship with Bill, then she probably believed she was the victorious one.

From what he'd seen the night before, Val was quite content in her own surroundings. Maybe, he surmised, she was one of those women who liked a monogamous relationship, but didn't want to give up her day-to-day independence.

The band began playing a slow country tune and Jeff put an arm around the sheriff's thin waist. Her frail body reminded him of his Aunt Primrose. Auntie Pim had loved to waltz, and he'd always made time for her when she'd put on the early vinyls of such populars as "The Tennessee Waltz" and her favorite, "The Rock and Roll Waltz." He could predict by the whiff of camphor and menthol that preceded his aged aunt into a room that she had applied a fresh layer of linament to her arthritic joints just so she could outlast a waltz or two.

"You got quiet on me, Talbot," prompted the sheriff.

He couldn't tell the sheriff what he'd been thinking about, so he introduced a subject that was sure to distract her. "I was wondering what that collection is that you're so secretive about."

"Don't go there."

"Why not? If you think you're going to shock me, you're wrong. I'm a picker, remember? You wouldn't believe some of the things I keep an eye out for, or the people who want them."

Her expression was thoughtful. Finally, she said, "Okay, but you have to promise you won't laugh."

"I can do that."

"Okay, I collect Barbie dolls."

Jeff was impressed. "If anyone laughs about that, then he doesn't know what Barbie is selling for these days."

"That's for sure. It's a good thing I only have myself to take care of. I have an image to maintain around here, though, so I don't let people know. If they aren't collectors, then they think you're nuts."

"I heard recently that the first Barbie can bring five figures. Do you spring for the rarer ones?"

"Don't have to. I had an uncle who predicted that they were going to be valuable. He started buying when the Number One Barbie came on the market in 1959." She paused, looked at him quizically.

"What's wrong?"

"I expected you to laugh when I mentioned my uncle."

"No, Ma'am. Gender has nothing to do with it. There are probably a lot of women right now who wish they had listened to him."

"That's for sure. He bought it all — dolls, outfits, Dream Houses, pink Corvettes, carrying cases — everything that had been manufactured. It's harder now to keep up with, and anyone who gets into collecting Barbie had better be prepared. Some of the dolls are limited edition and can only be purchased through the official club. Plus, you've got exclusive editions from companies like Avon — I told my Avon lady that I buy them for a niece in Iowa."

"Do you really have a niece in Iowa?"

"Hell, no. But my Avon lady doesn't have to know that. Anyway, when my uncle died, he left the entire collection to me. I'd planned to sell it off, even hauled it to a Barbie convention. I was hooked before you could say 'Halt! Police!' " She shook her head. "Nowadays, I plan my vacations around those conventions."

"Are you a completist?"

"I used to be, until I needed money to pay medical bills. It wasn't easy, selling off pieces. But what good would a doll collection be if I weren't around to enjoy it? So, I sold a Bob Mackie, a Vera Wang, and a —"

"*The* Vera Wang? Are you telling me that the top designers work for Barbie?"

"Yep. See what I mean? Barbie's big, Talbot."

As the song wound down, Jeff thought about Colleen McIvers, Vanessa Valentine, and Barbie — three independent, middle-aged women. Priceless.

Before they walked off the dance floor, the sheriff slipped him some folded papers. "I made a copy of Bill's inventory — the stolen items. Might come in handy when you're going through those boxes."

"Thanks."

"Thank *you* for the dance." She lowered her voice. "If either of Bill's women spills her guts, you be sure and let me know about it, you hear?"

"I always cooperate fully with the law . . . even when they don't charm me with the two-step."

"Your wife's a lucky lady, Talbot."

"Two-way street, Sheriff." He bowed, started back to his booth.

He was walking past the bar, heading back to the corner where his buddies were waiting, when someone touched his arm. It was Val.

"Miss Valentine. Val. Why don't you join us for a drink?"

"Thanks, but I'm not staying. I just wanted to thank you again for your kindness last night."

"I should be thanking you for giving me a look at all those antiques." He smiled. "It's always encouraging to meet a fellow collector."

"Don't forget to call me if you come across any pretty perfume bottles in the treasure you just acquired."

"I won't forget." He was more likely to forget where he lived before he'd lose track of who collected what. "Val, I'm really sorry for your loss."

"Thank you," she said, obviously touched by his sincerity. "We really did love each other, you know? Most people will never understand that."

He perched on the empty barstool next to her. "Did Bill have any enemies? Anyone who would have any reason to kill him?"

"I've been going crazy trying to figure that

one out. But I can't think of any one person. You know something, though? I keep going back to how he acted over the Internet. Do you think he saw something? Did you know that part of his collection was stolen a few years ago?"

"That's what I heard." Jeff refrained from telling her that he'd wondered the same thing, that he was in fact going to check Bill's computer files for that very clue.

"If you need me to do anything from this end, just call. I'd like to help."

"I'll do that."

"So, Colleen is using your antiques knowledge? Is that the only tie you have to this, or are you an undercover cop?"

"I guess it's no secret. I'm a former FBI agent. I used to track down stolen art, that sort of thing. Makes me a natural for this one, I suppose."

"What made you leave law enforcement? And don't tell me the antiques are more valuable."

"Not more valuable, just less scarce than the stolen stuff. I get my hands on a lot more of them now." He glanced at the booth, where his three buddies were putting on their jackets. "I'd better say good night. Although we drove up in my car, those three would leave me to walk."

"If they do, I'll give you a ride home."

"Thanks, but I'd never hear the end of that one."

Jeff awoke Sunday morning, anxious to return home. Typically, the men would go out on the water one last time, then eat lunch, clean up the cabin, and part ways.

Today, Jeff decided to skip the fishing. This proved, once and for all, that he wasn't a True Angler. He knew it, even before the others pointed it out.

After he'd told his fishing buddies good-bye, he tackled the job of loading the woodie for the trip home. The added cargo that was Bill's lures presented a logistical challenge and, with no small amount of effort and finesse, Jeff finally got everything packed into the station wagon.

After that, he swept the cabin's pine floors, took out the garbage, wiped down the counters, and made a final check for anything he might have left behind. He knew that the others would do the same, and he felt a twinge of loneliness when he realized that the feeling of closure came in shutting down the cabin together. He hoped he hadn't made a mistake by deciding to leave early.

He drove down the path, frequently

glancing in his rearview mirror to see if any of the guys had started back up from the river. But this proved fruitless, and he pulled onto the highway and headed toward the Rhodes home.

The maid answered the door. "Mrs. Rhodes said you'd be back today. She's napping right now, but told me to wake her when you arrived."

"It's not necessary to disturb her. I'll just be a few minutes."

"Mister, I need this job. If she told me —"

"How about a compromise? Allow me to get the computer work out of the way, then you can wake her when I'm ready to leave."

She thought a moment. "Are you working on anything that might help find Mr. Rhodes's killer?"

"Could turn out that way."

"I respected Mr. Rhodes." She glanced over her shoulder. "I'll give you thirty minutes."

"I'll only need ten."

Jeff punched a button and waited anxiously for the computer to boot up. Its chirping and whirring reverberated in the cold silence of the basement, and he prayed that the sounds wouldn't carry upstairs and set off some sort of alarm in Tanya's sub-conscious. Something like "man on board," or "red-blooded male in the building." He wondered how long it had taken Bill to grow tired of the relationship. He also wondered why the man had stayed married to her. Jeff suspected that it might be a lot cheaper than the alternative, and he thanked his own lucky stars that he would never have to go through that sort of misery. Rather than growing apart, he and Sheila were always discovering new and intriguing things about each other, things that both were interested in, things that fed the spark.

He withdrew a sheet of paper from his pocket, unfolded it, and spread it on the desk. He hoped he could decipher his notes and apply Sheila's instructions successfully.

He double-clicked the E-mail icon, and a screen popped up with the option to con-nect. He was in luck. Bill had checked "save password." Without that, he'd have been screwed. He hit Enter and waited.

When the screen appeared, several new messages were delivered to the Inbox. He minimized the screen without looking at them, and opened the Internet program.

Once that screen appeared, he clicked "Favorites" on the menu, and Bill's on-line list dropped down. Several folders appeared, followed by a subject list of Web sites. Jeff scrolled through the names, looking for anything that might be helpful. He passed on those with titles like "Fishing Guides," "Washington Waters," "Bait Shops," and homed in on the ones that appeared to be more promising.

A check into a folder titled "ID" listed around two dozen Web sites that featured antique fishing memorabilia; one with the name "Promote Fish" had links to pages offering promotional material. Another, titled "Buy Fish" listed sites from which aquarium fish could be purchased.

From there it got complicated. The deeper he dug, the more cryptic the names became until he wondered if Bill had at one time been a Navajo code talker for the military.

Jeff began to approach the task more systematically, opening folders, then opening folders within folders, eventually ignoring the strings of numbers and letters that served as folder names, checking the intricate infrastructure for something, anything, that might tell him what he was looking for.

And that's when he found himself in familiar territory. He clicked on a URL and was taken to an eBay auction page that depicted a Heddon Dowagiac lure in its original box. At the top of the page, in red letters, it read: This sale has ended.

He went back to the list and clicked on another. Same thing, an eBay page stating that the sale had ended.

He wondered why Bill had saved all these Web pages. Was he the seller? The buyer? Did he suspect that the lures were reproductions? Did he suspect that the lures were the ones that had been stolen from him?

Jeff doubted it. If they had been, Bill would have called the sheriff, and the sheriff would have told Jeff. More to the point, Internet fraud was a federal offense. The FBI, or the postal service, or both would now be on the case.

Jeff considered going through all the pages right then to cross-check the data. But a glance into the first couple of folders revealed dozens of pages. Just opening them for the purposes of forwarding would be a time-eater. No, he would work on the details after he got home.

He moved quickly, forwarding dozens of links to Sheila's E-mail address so that he could get done and get out.

When that chore was complete, he went back to the computer's E-mail program and skimmed through the column of folders on the left side of the screen until he found one with a name that stirred his curiosity. He quickly checked one of the messages, found Bill's E-mail address, and made a note of it.

Then he remembered that Sheila had some sort of nickname she used when bidding on eBay listings, and he surmised that Bill had one, too. He opened a couple of E-mails until he found one that notified the recipient of an auction win. He clicked a link that was included in the letter, and the Internet screen opened, revealing an eBay page for an antique lure.

On a whim, he checked the stolen item list that the sheriff had given him earlier. The information on the Web page seemed to match that on the inventory sheet.

He opened another E-mail, tried the same thing with another link. Ditto. But when he read over that letter again to see if it held any further information, he discovered that it had been delivered to a different nickname. He jotted this down, as well.

He repeated this process several more times, and each time he came up with yet another nickname.

A red flag went up in his brain.

It made sense that on-line buyers and sellers would want some anonymity. But why did Bill have several?

It didn't add up. *If these are Bill's stolen*

lures, Jeff thought, *then why has he been paying hefty sums to get them back?*

He scrolled back up the list to the stack of icons, searched for the top of the heap, and stared at the folder's name. It was a two-word title: MINE AGAIN

PART TWO

THE LURE

᛭

"I am, out of the ladies' company
like a fish out of the water."
— Thomas Shadwell
A True Widow, 1679

CHAPTER THIRTEEN

৯৭

SNAGGING: Attempting to take fish with a hook and line in such a way that the fish does not voluntarily take the hook(s) in its mouth.
— *Washington State Department of Fish and Wildlife*

The drive home was tedious, but Jeff was happy that he'd gotten out of the Rhodes home before Tanya had awakened from her nap.

He pulled into the carriage house, grabbed his duffel bag from the back seat, and went inside, thankful that he wouldn't have to worry about unloading the fishing gear or putting away the foodstuffs. Greer would automatically see to that.

Sheila ran down the service stairs and into his arms. Jeff wasn't sure how she knew it was him entering the house and not Greer, but she had a particular sense about the goings-on in the big old place.

"Hey, stranger," she said, "you look good in a rugged sort of way."

He stroked the sparse beard. "What do you think? Should I keep it?"

She stood back, studied him intently. "I'm not sure which way I like better. Before you stopped shaving last week, you looked adorable — like Kevin Kline in *In and Out.* Now, here you are, all rough and sexy like he was in *French Kiss.*" She lowered her voice. "I have a beret upstairs . . ."

Jeff muttered the few French phrases he knew. Maybe he wasn't the sexy character in the movie, but his moves were enough to keep the mood going and lead to an amorous encounter.

Afterward, they visited until it turned dark outside, and filled each other in on their weekends.

At length he said, "I'm starving, but I'm beat, too. Is there —"

"You don't need to say another word. I'll bring dinner up here, and we can lie in bed, watch a movie or two, then turn in?"

He pulled her close. "There's only one drawback."

"What might that be?" She kissed his ear.

"You'll be gone for an hour."

"Not true. I didn't know when you'd be home, so I planned accordingly." She hopped up and threw a cozy fleece robe over her slender body. "Back in a jif."

After she left, he went to the vanity area of his lavatory where he kept a coffee station set up — a true sign if ever there was one of his java fanatacism. He put on a pot to brew, then went to Sheila's office and made a quick check of her E-mail to make sure he'd forwarded the Web pages properly from Bill's computer.

He was relieved to find that he'd done the job right. Following every link to its original Web site was going to be a challenging and time-consuming task. Add to that the job of figuring out what, if anything, it had to do with Bill's murder, and it moved to a new level altogether. He was debating signing in and getting a start on the job, but he knew that he'd get too caught up in it. It wasn't called a web for nothing. Besides, Sheila would be back up any minute. He closed the program and headed back to the bedroom, promising himself he'd get up early the next day and work on the links.

He'd just put *You've Got Mail* in the VCR when Sheila walked in with an enormous picnic basket and a red checkered table-cloth. She spread the cloth on the bed, then unpacked fried chicken, potato salad, sliced tomatoes, a relish tray, fluffy angel biscuits, and apple pie. Jeff poured two cups of coffee and joined his wife.

They watched a second movie — *Runaway Bride* — laughed till they cried, ate almost the entire pie, and fell asleep so completely and comfortably entwined that only the jaws of life could have separated them.

The next morning, Greer discreetly slipped into their room with a carafe of strong coffee and a large basket of pastries.

And who said butlers weren't needed in the twenty-first century?

Jeff hadn't left instructions for Greer to serve breakfast at a particular time, though, so his day began an hour later than he'd intended for it to. Typical Monday morning irritations followed closely on the coattails of the late start: He cut himself shaving, spilled coffee on his sweater, and had to inch the woodie through traffic because of a detour that looped him around the Space Needle.

When he finally arrived at the warehouse, he walked to the back to examine the items that had been damaged in Thursday night's truck accident. He picked up a corner of a rolled-up moving quilt and the broken pieces inside rattled like bones in a gunny sack.

An image of Bill revisited his mind for the hundredth time, but the reality of murder simply wouldn't register now that Jeff was back in his real world. It was as if he'd experienced one of those fragmented nightmares in which people died and were resurrected only to laugh at you later when you told them over the phone or over a beer that they were killed in your dreams the previous night, and that it was so real you had to see them to make sure they were okay.

He poured coffee from his Thermos and, using a folded sheet of paper from his pad as a coaster on a Chippendale side table, he sank into a leather chair worn soft as butter and began crunching numbers.

The loss of goods he'd suffered in the wreck was substantial, but he'd be able to make things balance out if he played his cards right. He would spend a little more time evaluating what he had, then put together a laundry list of items that might warrant a call to an auction house. There was the possibility of parlaying this into enough income to carry him for a couple of years — but it would require some shrewd business moves on his part.

Blanche had first choice, of course, after Jeff set aside what he wanted for personal reasons, and she could always be counted on to offer him the best prices. She wouldn't try to take him to the cleaners, and besides, even the huge warehouse that was now All Things Old couldn't accommodate everything he'd acquired in one fell swoop. The place was already packed, with a steady stream of pickers carting things in so that consumers might enjoy an astounding choice.

Jeff drank his coffee as he sorted through photos. He chose a couple depicting some real treasures to show to Blanche in her office and put the rest in a manila envelope for her to take home and peruse that night.

Another day like this one, then three marathon days of packing and moving and unpacking the small stuff, and the weekend would be upon him. That was when he, Sam, Maura, and Maura's fiancé, Darius (who was, fortunately, a plumber) were going to meet at the two houses and salvage all the architectural elements. Those items alone — the brass doorknobs with their elaborate backplates and matching door hinges, the Victorian spandrels and scrolled corner brackets, the vintage light fixtures, the pedestal sinks and clawfoot tubs — more than made up for what the contents of the two buildings had cost him.

There was no denying that he had a month's worth of work to accomplish in six days. He'd be damned surprised if the whole plan came off without a hitch.

He'd worked out a barter with the Carvers on this one when he'd taken them to see the properties a week and a half earlier. Maura and Darius were in the planning stages of building a home and wanted the porcelain from two of the five bathrooms. Sam laid claim to a toolbox that he had spotted in the basement of Building Two. The box had been made in the late 1800s out of three woods — ebony, purplewood, and rosewood, with a matching set of planes in eight sizes, all trimmed in etched brass. It had undeniably been built by an artisan, and included in the box was the craftsmen's poem by St. Francis of Assissi. It epitomized Sam Carver's approach to his livelihood:

He who works with his hands is a laborer.
He who works with his hands and his head is a craftsman.
He who works with his hands and his head and his heart is an artist.

A pricey trade, that one, but worth the care and knowledge that Sam would bring to the weekend project. Besides, you did things for friends that couldn't be calculated with dollar signs, knowing that the same would be done for you if need be.

Sam had been near tears as he admired the case and its treasures. Then, in keeping with his personality, had turned to Jeff and said with mock seriousness, "I'm going to take a shaving on this deal, but since it's you . . ."

Jeff grinned at the memory, and at Sam's wood-shaving pun.

The rumble of a truck's engine jogged his thoughts, brought him back to the present. *That'll be the moving crew,* he thought, surprised that they'd made the round-trip with yet another load so quickly. Blanche had enlisted two more men for him, and he'd asked her to let the first crew know that they could join in as soon as they'd made arrangements for a truck. It would cut into his profits, but he was having twinges of panic over meeting his contract deadline with the old woman's nephew.

As the team unloaded furniture and unwrapped the protective packing quilts, Jeff checked the items against his inventory sheets. His goal was to get together a preliminary list and deliver it to Blanche, along with the Polaroids he'd been snapping, before calling it a day.

He glanced at his watch and realized he'd barely looked up since his lunch of leftovers from the fishing trip — Vienna sausages, crackers, and Sheila's cowboy cookies — four hours earlier.

But just as he thought he was ready to leave, he found himself drawn to the corner where the cartons from Bill's basement were stacked. He knew that to wade through, weed out, categorize, and evaluate would be a hell of a task, one that would require his full mental capacities. Curiosity got the best of him, though. Using his pocketknife, he slit the tape in assembly-line fashion and began sorting through Bill's collection.

He emptied carton after carton, amazed at how organized the collection was. Each box held a specific brand of lures — Heddon, Shakespeare, Pfleuger, Creek Chub. When he unwrapped the contents of the fifth box, he jumped. The flies that had startled him were so lifelike he thought at first that the container was infested. He hadn't seen very many of the Keeling flies in his years as a picker, but they were easy to identify. Nobody, by Jeff's estimation, could touch Fred Keeling's expertise.

There was a common thread — literally — among those lures of Bill's that sported either bucktails or feathers. Expertly tied into the center of each of the tufts used by fly-tyers to camouflage the hooks was a single silky strand of red embroiderer's floss. It didn't take Jeff long to determine that it was Bill's discreet way of identifying the pieces in his extensive and valuable collection, and he wondered whether Bill had been doing this all along. He would have to check the computer files when he got home and determine whether the eBay items had the trademark red thread.

He also wondered whether the lures that didn't have deer hair or feathers had some sort of discerning mark. He examined a few and, although he thought an extra, identifying mark had been added, he really couldn't be sure without a magnifying glass.

His picker's kit, which was in the car, had a small magnifying glass, as well as the other tools used to check authenticity, search for maker's marks, and narrow the field where age and value were key: black light, jeweler's loop, angled mirrors, even pencils — whose erasers could be rubbed against metal to help determine whether or not a piece was sterling silver. If the eraser removed tarnish, you likely had a promising treasure.

He hadn't brought the kit in from the car, since he wasn't planning to do any detailed investigating this early in the game. He made a mental note to examine the wooden lures later.

He moved on, opening cartons and making a surreptitious examination of the lures, becoming more and more astounded at the value before him.

With seven cartons aside, he pulled back the flaps of number eight only to discover what appeared to be the personal keepsakes of a teenaged girl. He began unpacking diaries, yearbooks, albums bulging with newspaper clippings, and bundles of letters tied with pastel ribbons — pink, lavender, yellow.

He withdrew a plain black frame from the box, tilted it toward the light.

The photo it contained depicted a young woman who looked amazingly like Nancy Kerrigan — slender and fit, with black hair. The girl was wearing black — a tanktop and satin running shorts — as if to create the most dramatic backdrop for the large gold medallion that hung from a red, white, and blue grosgrain ribbon around her neck. She held a trophy that was easily half her size.

Jeff tried to remember whether Bill had ever mentioned having a daughter, but he didn't recall such a reference ever being made.

More digging in the box unearthed a couple of trophies (much smaller than the one in the photo) and a number of presentation boxes — each containing a beribboned medal.

He thumbed through one of the albums, skimmed a couple of newspaper articles, pieced together the puzzle. He reached for a phone, then remembered where he was. It was time to call it a day anyway, he decided, so he locked up the warehouse, and walked to the nearest pay phone.

After fumbling with his wallet and finding the business card he'd put there, he stabbed the numbers, then waited anxiously.

"McIvers."

"Sheriff, it's Jeff Talbot."

"Hey, fishin' bud. You've jumped ship by now, I reckon."

"Afraid so, but you'll be glad to hear that I might have a hell of a lead on your killer. Turns out, one of these boxes we got from Bill's basement wasn't his. I just got a blast from the past of a teenage girl.

"She looked quite a bit different eight or ten years ago," he continued. "Muscular, in a figure-skater sort of way. I've got photos, BP-BS —"

"Wait a minute. What the hell's BP-BS?"

"Sorry. 'Before platinum, before silicone.' She had black hair and . . . well, let's just say her figure didn't prevent those medals from resting flat against her chest.

"Here's the kicker, though. All these trophies and medals belong to a girl by the name of Tanya Price, aka, your grieving widow, Tanya Rhodes. That was her name before she married Bill Rhodes, easy enough to verify. Wait till you see the photos, Sheriff. She competed in a very interesting sport throughout high school and college."

"Interesting? How so?"

"The Widow Rhodes was a javelin thrower."

The sheriff missed a beat, then said, "Bill was killed with a fishing spear."

"Exactly."

"Looks like I've got an alibi to try and crack."

"Let me know what you turn up." He rang off, walked the two blocks along the harbor toward Blanche's shop, leaving behind the headaches of the warehouse and the nagging worries over Bill's murder.

"Jeffrey! I was beginning to think you'd

forgotten all about me." Blanche was sitting cross-legged on the floor, surrounded by several open reference books on antiques.

The sight warmed him. There weren't many women in their seventies who would attempt such a feat. Blanche always started at one of the two large French writing desks that occupied her office but, if an item proved elusive, she frequently got serious by moving the whole research process to ground level.

He offered a hand, and she took it, then dropped into her office chair like the little red-headed rag doll she was. He tossed two photos on the desk in front of her.

She studied first one, then the other. She shook her head. "Jeffrey, you must be more worn out than I am. You took two pictures of the same piece of furniture."

He sat opposite her and grinned broadly. "They're twins, Blanche. Two of them, as identical as Leigh and Leslie Keno."

"I don't believe it." She studied the photos of the little corner cabinets, her eyes darting back and forth between the two. "Thank God *these* weren't in the accident.

"I'm not sure whether they're French or English," she went on. "The marquetry makes me think French. See how the design of each inlaid vase is tall, slender, elegant?

But the rest says late nineteenth-century English." Blanche looked up. "Do you know how rare these are?"

"I had a hunch."

"That old woman *was* insane, wasn't she? Did you see the article about her in the paper? Sick, wouldn't go to the doctor, appearing as if she needed money. And here she was, holding on to a fortune."

"That's easier for me to believe than her half-wit nephew, selling this stuff to me for a fraction of what it's really worth. But my conscience is clear. I tried to get him to call a reputable auction house. He didn't want to mess with it."

"All the better for us, I say." She picked up the manila envelope. "I'll curl up with this tonight," she said, squeezing the fat package to her breast as if it were a juicy romance novel. "I'll choose what I want and have an offer for you by tomorrow afternoon."

Jeff nodded, wished he had half the energy as Blanche Appleby. He attributed her success to her quick, sharp mind and her instinct for what the public wanted. She could be the poster girl for "No Fear."

"I'm sorry, Jeffrey. I should've offered you some tea. Or some coffee?"

"Thanks, but I'd better get moving. Greer

took the day off after making us a gallon of coffee for the morning, and Sheila asked me to drop by Pike Place and pick up some salmon for dinner."

Blanche sat back, obviously happy. "I had the best time visiting with Sheila while you were gone. She's quite the hostess, and that bread pudding with blackberry sauce? Out of this world!"

"Don't I know it." Jeff patted his stomach. "I'm going to have to start working out more, I guess. I don't dare push away from the table, or she'll think I don't appreciate her."

"It'll be worth a few more trips to the gym, I can say that."

"You'll get no argument from me." Jeff rose. "I'll drop by tomorrow when I'm finished at the warehouse."

Blanche tapped the manila envelope. "I'll rob a bank in the meantime."

Pike Place Market had changed some since Jeff had first visited it as a child but, overall, the atmosphere was the same. He was standing near the south end, mesmerized by the bright neon signs that hung from the rafters, when a fish vendor sailed a salmon through the air not ten inches in front of his nose. The stunt was as much to capture the attention of passing consumers as it was to entertain the tourists. Jeff arched a brow. He wondered if they'd mistaken him for a tourist, which was likely, since he had appeared so awestruck by the carnival-like surroundings.

A couple of kids scrambled off the bronze back of the resident charity piggy bank — a life-sized rendition named Rachel — and hurried over to watch the "flying" fish. Feeling generous, Jeff fed a ten spot through the bank's slot and was warmed by the sense of community the gesture gave him.

He was glad he'd left the woodie parked at the warehouse. He would make better time on foot, what with the corporate crowd clogging the arteries leading out of downtown. He strode along, welcoming the crisp air and the chance to stretch his legs in earnest.

He didn't get down here too often anymore, so he took advantage of this opportunity by soaking up the atmosphere, working his way through the knots of busy shoppers, cutting across the wide lanes to select items from various merchants — a baguette from the baker, a bundle of fall cuttings from the florist, some magazines from the newsstand. He should do this more often, he thought. Not so much as to cross the boundaries of Greer's duties — he didn't want their employee to misinterpret that he wasn't doing a good job — but enough to stay in touch with all the good things his town had to offer.

He purchased the salmon last, watched the young man wrap and tie the silver and coral fish in white butcher paper, then headed back to his car a few blocks away.

It was dusk by the time he arrived in Queen Anne. He enjoyed this time, liked to drive north, up Queen Anne Avenue, and watch as the shops' lights glowed and warmed the gray sidewalks like those in the paintings by Thomas Kinkade.

He turned, nosed the woodie along residential streets cramped with vehicles. So many of the historical homes of his neighborhood had been converted into apartment complexes, and parking was always at a premium. Fortunately for him, his ancestors hadn't relinquished an inch of ground. Still standing on his property was the original carriage house, which provided the shelter he needed to protect the woodie's finish.

He took the corner where his house stood and suddenly felt cold. The only light he saw was a blue glow from the third-floor window of Sheila's office. The house as a whole looked gloomy without the golden light that usually emanated from within. The red brick, the warm gold and ivory shades of trim paint, all lay flat. He pulled into the driveway, straining as he did so to see if there was a light on in the kitchen. Nothing. The place was as dark and gray as the warehouse from which he'd just come.

Sheila should be downstairs by now. She always allowed plenty of time to cook, and an equal amount of time to dress the table in crisp linens, polished silver, glittering crystal, and a centerpiece of her own creation. She believed in *dining,* not merely eating.

She should be busy preparing all those dishes she had planned to go with the salmon. It wasn't like her to become so wrapped up in the Internet that she lost all track of time.

He feared that she had taken ill but, if that were so, wouldn't she have called Greer on his cellphone? Or, if she had been hesitant to bother their butler on his day off, she could have phoned Blanche at All Things Old, who, in turn, would have immediately dispatched Trudy to the warehouse to fetch Jeff.

What if she had fallen? He had warned her

time and time again to slow down as she shot up and down the flights of stairs that connected the house's four stories.

His mind struggled with itself, one side telling him to hit the panic button, the other telling him that there had to be a reasonable explanation.

He didn't bother with the garage but rather stopped the car at the back steps. He grabbed the shopping bags and darted up the steps to the door, where he juggled packages and fumbled with the house key. In an effort to maintain balance, he bumped against the door.

It pushed open.

He checked, discovered that the lock was activated but whoever had closed the door hadn't pushed tightly enough for it to click into the chamber. He flipped the light switch with his elbow, deposited the packages on the long, empty refectory table that served as Sheila's culinary workstation. By now, the table should have been equipped like an assembly line: dessert with the proper china for serving it at one end, bread basket lined with a linen cloth, an array of washed vegetables awaiting the magic of the chef in residence.

"Sheila?" He walked from the kitchen, hitting switches as he went, glancing into rooms: library, dining room, his study, the parlor.

"Sheila?" He called again as he bounded up the stairs to the second floor. There, he checked the master bedroom, both dressing rooms, both bathrooms.

"Sheila!" More urgent this time. "Where in the hell are you?"

Taking the next flight of stairs two at a time, he arrived breathless on the landing.

He paused, told himself to calm down. She was in her office, he assured himself, locked in a heated discussion in some chat room or trapped in the innermost weavings of the Web. "C'mon, hon, answer me," he called as he made his way down the long corridor. "I'm too damned old to be playing hide and seek."

But when he arrived in her office, he found it empty, quiet, except for the rhythmic wash of waves and the calls of gulls that were part of the lighthouse screen saver.

His heart pounded.

He went to the other end of the third floor, to the adjoining bedrooms she'd converted into her own personal antiques shop, and flung open the first door he came to. Dark. He flipped the switch and the light — sharp, glaring — bounced off an array of items that awaited selection by the mistress of the house. Some were displayed as if arranged for a shop window, others lined along shelving, still others in gift wrap so as to offer a surprise to a woman who couldn't leave the premises.

He went through the connecting door, knowing already that she wouldn't be on the other side.

He ran to the small door that opened up onto a narrow staircase that led up to the widow's walk. He couldn't recall the last time Sheila had gone up there. It was too much like going outside for her, but he decided to check anyway.

He opened the door. The stairwell was so dark that he couldn't get his bearings. No type of lighting had been installed in the passage leading up top to the square landing, the vantage point from which Jeff's grandfather's mother had watched for the return of her husband — watched, even after word arrived that his ship had capsized off the coast of India.

Was that it? Had Sheila gotten caught up in the notion that he'd been away too long? Had she gone up there as a last-ditch effort to urge him home?

Jeff couldn't fathom it, the notion that Sheila was up there, but he was running out of options. He groped his way to the top of the stairs and threw open the door.

Moonlight illuminated the tiny windowed square. No Sheila.

What was left? The basement, he considered doubtfully. His mind speculated wildly at the events that might have driven her down there. His heart pounded harder against his chest wall.

Logic teased him, told him that maybe she'd decided to unearth some just-remembered painting, or accent table, or an item from her past. He descended staircase after staircase, soothed and panicked by turns, hoping she was in the basement yet chilled by the fact that she hadn't come upstairs at the sounds of him in the house.

She'd always amazed him with her skill for identifying any sound coming from any level of their home. It didn't matter which part of the house she was in at the time, she had such a *connection* to the structure. Jeff attributed this to the fact that she'd become one with the place, perhaps even more so than with him. He may be her husband, but this was her *sanctuary*.

If she wasn't in the basement, then he knew of only one more option in the massive house. It was an option he dreaded.

She wasn't in the basement. Gulping air,

he climbed the stairs back to ground level. Only one area remained.

The secret passageways.

When Jeff was only seven years old, he had discovered a hidden staircase in the massive Victorian home — a staircase that had been unknown to Primrose Talbot. The woman couldn't wrap her mind around the notion that a mere boy had stumbled upon something so important — something that she had never come across. To add insult to injury, Grandfather Talbot had announced, with obvious pride in the boy, that the house must really like Jeff to have shared its secret and that the property would be signed over to him as soon as he became of age.

Although Auntie Pim was aware of her father's adherence to the old ways, which dictated that the men in the family should own the real estate, she had been openly stunned by this turn of events. Jeff, reveling in a child's triumph, didn't realize until years later how hurt she had been. But he recognized in time that she was the working force that held the mansion together, and when the attorney brought around documents giving him sole ownership of the property, Jeff had simply refused to sign. Only after Auntie Pim's stroke had he taken the Talbot reins.

He hadn't been through the maze of hidden corridors in years. *I wish Greer were here,* he thought as he made his way to the nearest opening that led behind the walls of the house. Greer was familiar with the maze because he often used it just as Sir Anthony Hopkins' character had used similar passageways in *Remains of the Day.* But Jeff didn't expect his butler for another three hours.

He pushed against a portion of paneled wall in the library, groped along the wall inside until he found a button. He pressed it, and a soft, dim light illuminated the narrow hall.

As he walked through these arteries of his house, he began to feel encouraged by the realization that Sheila could actually be somewhere inside the walls. Perhaps something had caused her to panic, had driven her into the tightest possible recesses of the house. She would feel safe here, he surmised, she would welcome the narrow corridors, welcome the feel of the close walls wrapping themselves around her.

He called her name, got only an echo.

He moved faster, thankful that the lighting system of the hidden corridors was wired to work every fixture on every floor.

He covered the first floor, peering down

the capillaries that shot from the main artery. He glanced down the staircase that led to the basement, then continued on, covering every open space as if he were liquid — flowing, reaching into each conceivable inch.

But Sheila wasn't there.

He emerged, gasping, and ran down the flights of stairs, rechecking every floor, yelling Sheila's name as he descended, having it bounce back to him unanswered. He moved swiftly, gulping the void and choking against the knowledge that he would not find his wife.

He needed help.

Breathless, his chest heaving, he grabbed the cordless phone from the kitchen wall and punched in Greer's cell number after locating it on the cork bulletin board. Walking through the tiny mud room toward the back door, he opened it and glued his spine to the doorway as if to keep from collapsing. He placed one foot in the house, the other on the outer stoop, and waited for Greer to pick up.

"My God, Sheila," he cried into the darkness, "where are you?"

CHAPTER FOURTEEN

৯৯

O, God, thy sea is so great and my boat is so small.
— *Ancient prayer of Breton fishermen*

"It's my fault." Pacing, Greer ran slim fingers through his short black hair.

The butler's slender body was tense, and Jeff attributed this to some inner core of professionalism struggling against the raw need to give way to emotion.

His own body was at that same stage, and he told himself over and over to keep a grip. He'd be of no help in finding Sheila if he fell apart.

He clamped his free hand on the young butler's shoulder. "No, it's not. Don't say that again." With his other hand, he held the phone to his ear, waiting for the police dispatcher to come back on the line.

"But I would have been here if I hadn't taken the day off. I would have —"

"Greer. First of all, you can't work seven days a week. I'd see to that, even if Sheila were bedridden." A glimpse of that future possibility flashed in his mind, and he erased the thought. "A large part of your duties is to run all of Sheila's errands. That's not going to change. I don't know what drove her to leave the house, but it could've happened during a thirty-minute window while you were at the cleaners or the grocery store."

Greer appeared ready to protest again, but Jeff lifted a finger, brought the phone nearer his mouth.

"Mister, uh . . . Talbot? You still there?"

"Of course I'm still here. My wife's missing, for God's sake."

"Not technically, sir. Your wife being missing, I mean. Unless there are extenuating circumstances, a person has to have been gone —"

"But there are extenuating circumstances. There's illness involved. She doesn't leave the house."

"Okay." The dispatcher exhaled. "I'll send someone over."

Before Jeff could respond, he heard the buzz of the dial tone. "*Damn* them." He slammed the phone into its cradle. "They don't know what this is like."

He leaned against the wall, willed himself to think. He wondered if a phone call had rattled Sheila, set her off somehow. He punched an arrow key on the phone pad, checked caller ID. The last number listed was that of the cellphone he'd used to call her on just before Bill's funeral.

He punched Call and his telephone automatically dialed the number on the display.

"Hello?"

"Judge? It's Jeff."

"Hey, old man," the Judge said enthusiastically. "Didn't you get enough of my company at the cabin? Not to mention my poker money."

"I need help, Judge. Sheila's gone."

"Gone? But that's . . ."

"Impossible. I know. Thing is, I don't know whether the damned dispatcher understood. No telling how long it'll take to get someone over here to help."

Jeff heard crickets chirp in the silence.

"What about Gordy? Have you called him yet?"

"No. I thought it would be best to get the locals here first."

"You're right. Want me to put in a call, light a fire under them?"

"Would you? I'm going nuts here."

"Damn right, I will. I've got a captain who owes me anyway. He'll send some extra officers to your house in under ten, or I'll know the reason why."

"Okay, and I'll call Gordy."

"Do you think he's back in Chicago yet?"

"I don't know. He's supposed to be back there sometime today. Judge, thanks. I . . ." Jeff fought to retain composure.

"It's the least I can do. Keep me posted." He rang off.

Jeff replaced the receiver more gently this time, looked at Greer who was waiting anxiously. "We'll have help here in a few minutes."

Greer exhaled. "I'll make coffee, sir."

Jeff watched his butler as he methodically went through the steps for brewing coffee — grinding the beans, lining the basket, filling the carafe with cold water, pouring it into the reservoir. At least Greer had something constructive to do, something to occupy his hands, his thoughts, if only for a few moments. Jeff felt a twinge of envy.

Greer bolted toward the butler's pantry just off the kitchen and, soon, Jeff heard the opening and closing of cabinet doors, the clinking of silver and china, the crackle of packages. Although he and Sheila rarely had company, Greer was always prepared with some sort of finger foods that could be set out at the drop of a hat. Jeff didn't expect that the officers would partake, but he left Greer to the busyness of preparation.

He picked up the phone, punched in a number that he didn't need to look up.

Gordy Easthope picked up halfway through the second ring, and Jeff figured he'd waited for caller ID to register.

"Talbot, you old reprobate," he said by way of a greeting. "It's about damned time you called with a fishing report."

"Gordy." Jeff's voice was strained. He tried to continue, but couldn't find the words. The sound of his ex-partner's voice brought on a wash of security, and Jeff felt as if he'd been holding it together just long enough to turn everything over to the most capable man he knew. That, combined with the thought of having to repeat the words, "Sheila's missing," brought on such a wave of emotion that he was rendered speechless.

"What's wrong, bud?"

"Where are you?" Jeff measured out the words.

"Just leaving O'Hare, why? What's going on?"

"It's Sheila." Jeff's voice cracked. "She's . . . she's not here."

He heard the shuffling of papers on the other end of the phone, followed by the blare of a horn, and the shrillness of a siren. Gordy was on the move.

Jeff heard more shuffling, then Gordy yelled over the squall. "There's a nonstop in fifteen. I'll be on it. Cops at your place yet?"

"Soon. The Judge is slicing through bureaucratic red tape for me."

"Good. Meanwhile, have Greer call everybody he knows — butcher, store clerks, other house employees. Have him use his cellphone. Keep either that or the house line clear at all times, in case she tries to call in. Get every damn person in the neighborhood looking.

"I'll have an agent pick me up at Sea-Tac." He paused, killed the siren. "Jeff?"

"Yeah?"

"Hang in there, buddy." Gordy broke the connection.

As Jeff replaced the phone, Greer entered the room. "Sir, the police have arrived. They are waiting for you in the library."

Jeff nodded, hurried toward the front of the house.

Two officers — one male, one female — stood near the fireplace where Greer had a fire going. They turned as Jeff entered the room. He glanced at their sleeves, then extended his hand to the ranking officer. "I appreciate your coming so quickly."

"I'm Sergeant Tom Wyatt." He shook Jeff's hand. "This is Officer Hart. Larrabee didn't leave us much choice."

"Have a seat." Jeff indicated the couch.

The uniformed pair sat. Sergeant Wyatt said, "The Judge told me you weren't exaggerating when you said your wife wouldn't wander off without good reason."

Jeff stood by the fireplace. He was afraid that if he sat down he'd fall into some sort of black hole. He took a photo of Sheila from the mantle, gripped it tightly as he gazed at the image of the smiling woman.

"Did your dispatcher fill you in?"

Wyatt turned to his partner. "Hart, you talked to dispatch, right?"

"Yes, sir." She looked at Jeff, and he got the distinct impression that she pegged him as an abusive husband. "He just said that your wife wasn't on any medication, wasn't under a doctor's care —"

"*Isn't.*" Jeff's jaw tightened. "Don't use past tense when you refer to my wife."

"Sorry. I'm used to working homicide."

"Then what the hell are you doing here?"

Hart looked up questionably at Wyatt.

"Mr. Talbot," Wyatt said, "did you and your wife have some sort of disagreement?"

"No." Jeff shook his head, muttered, "For God's sake."

"No problems in, say, the last few months?"

"I said, no."

"Isn't it possible that she went for a walk, or left to meet a girlfriend for a drink. Have you called her friends?"

Jeff slammed his fist against the wall. "Haven't you been listening? My wife is *agoraphobic*. She —"

"I understand —"

"The hell you do. My wife has an illness that has prevented her from leaving this house for the last five years. She doesn't *meet* friends for lunch. She doesn't *go* for walks. She doesn't even leave to go to the doctor, or the dentist, or the beauty shop. When she needs something, *anything*, I bring people in. *Get it through your heads, she does not leave these walls!*"

"There's no reason to yell, sir."

Jeff locked eyes with Wyatt, stared him down.

"Did the Judge tell you that I'm an FBI agent?" Jeff wasn't sure why he didn't say *former* agent. *Who cares?* He thought. He needed every possible advantage he could gain, for Sheila's sake.

Surprise swept over the sergeant's face,

then left just as quickly. "No. What difference does that make?"

"Put aside your prejudices, Sergeant, and realize that I'm not given to hysterics. I've had training. Listen to me when I say that this is a special case.

"My wife wandering around out there is no different from an Alzheimer's patient out there, or a four-year-old. Each of them would, at the very least, be disoriented, frightened. At the worst? You should know the answer to that one without my spelling it out. They would be in increasingly advancing stages of dementia, panic, fear. And so will my wife.

"You know what it's like here on Queen Anne," he continued. "One crowded street after another. One block of houses practically identical to the last. And to the next. Several streets are dead-ends. Others loop around to accommodate the hills. To someone who hasn't spent any time on these streets familiarizing himself with the layout, the landmarks, these houses are nothing more than cookie-cutter look-alikes — bungalow after bungalow, street after street.

"If my wife's disoriented enough, she may not even remember the name of our street. She sure as hell won't have her bear-

251

ings. Do you understand?"

"I'm beginning to, sir. I have two more officers outside. We'll grid off the hill, start knocking on doors." Wyatt reached for the photo.

Reluctantly, Jeff handed it over.

"Do you have more of these?"

Jeff looked at Greer, who nodded and hurried from the room. He returned with a small stack of photographs in varying sizes, handed it to the sergeant.

Officer Hart asked, "What was she wearing?"

"I left early this morning." Jeff again looked to Greer.

"When I left around nine, sir, she was in black twill pants with a two-piece sweater set: tan, white, and black stripes. Black loafers, hair pulled back with a black leather barrette."

The officer nodded as she wrote, then stood. "We'll let you know if we find anything."

Jeff started toward them. "I want to come with you. She'll respond better if I'm there."

The sergeant sighed. "Not a good idea, Mr. Talbot, and you know it. Besides, we need you to stay put. That way, if she comes home of her own accord, you'll be here.

And, if *we* find her, we'll know where to find *you*."

After a moment, Jeff nodded. He watched Greer lead the officers out of the room, listened for the front door to close, then went to the kitchen phone. He had one more call to make.

He found the listing in the small address book Sheila kept in a kitchen drawer and dialed the number for her sister, Karen. He'd be surprised if he caught her at home. Karen Gray was the exact opposite of Sheila and, as a photographer for *National Geographic*, she could be a dot anywhere on the globe.

The recording she'd left on her answering machine confirmed his suspicions. It said, "I'm shooting bats in Bolivia. What are you doing?"

He rang off without leaving a message. What could Karen do from a cave in South America?

"Greer," he called as he put on a jacket.

"Sir?"

"I need your cellphone."

Without comment, Greer pulled the slim black phone from his breast pocket and handed it to Jeff.

"If you hear *anything*, you call me."

"Yes, sir. Should I know where you're going, sir?"

He paused for a moment. "The water-front."

Greer smiled timidly. "I hope he's down there tonight."

"He will be." Jeff's confidence turned to determination. "He has to be."

The waterfront was either vacant or bus-tling by turns, depending upon which fer-ries were docking and unloading and which were only string-light skeletons moving across the dark waters of the bay. It was too late in the year for the usual outdoor con-certs, and fewer couples strolled arm-in-arm along the boardwalk. Ferry passengers rushed to get onboard and head home to Bremerton or Vashon Island, until the next morning when they would commute to the Emerald City and repeat the workweek pro-cess.

Jeff cruised slowly down Alaskan Way, peering into shadows, studying outlines of the occasional dark figures sitting on benches or leaning on dock moorings, searching for the one man who might help him scour the underbelly of the city for any thread of a lead on his wife.

Driving the woodie had its advantages. When Jeff wanted to be seen, the car was like a neon billboard. When he didn't, he used the SUV that he furnished Greer with for shopping and errands. Tonight, he needed neon. Lanny knew this about Jeff, knew the rarity of Jeff's night trips to the waterfront. If Lanny was down here, he'd make himself known. Or die trying.

This Jeff could count on, even though he had never known anyone for so long and at the same time known so little. The man had never given his last name, and Jeff had never entertained the notion of tracking it down. If nothing else, his FBI training had taught him that information was his best weapon, and he wasn't so stupid as to jeopardize his relationship with the best street informant he'd ever worked with — and that included his years with the Bureau.

Lanny was a picker. A *real* picker, some would say, not like Talbot the former agent who had come to the trade later in life with an inherited house full of inherited antiques and an uncanny knack for turning up good merchandise.

Lanny wasn't judgmental, and Jeff accredited this to his ability to recognize that at the core the two men were the same. They both loved their work and were passionate about preserving the past.

All similarity stopped there. While it was typically part of the picker personality to become so fascinated by *stuff* that he might very well forget about people, Lanny was both a picker and an observer. People and objects held equal value in his regard.

Jeff never knew whether he'd find Lanny driving the rust-eaten Ford, with its oxidized paint of a color and drabness similar to mud, or on foot combing through trash and acting more like a homeless bum than those who actually were.

Jeff studied an approaching vehicle with one of its two headlights hanging loose from the socket, like a naked bulb on a long cord. He wondered if its driver had still managed to avoid a traffic ticket, or whether he just paid them when they were delivered — much like utility bills and tax statements.

As they passed on the street, the two drivers locked eyes for a split second, then drove on. Jeff kept an eye on his rearview mirror, watched the truck turn and make its way north through the rows of parking spaces under the viaduct. Jeff pulled up to the warehouse where he'd spent the day, and positioned the woodie so that he could keep the pickup in his sights. He killed the lights and waited.

Lanny parked the truck diagonally among a group of cars, then jogged toward the woodie. He was rail thin, and his clothes hung loosely on a frame perpetually slouched. If Jeff didn't know better, he'd think the man never got enough to eat. As he always did when he saw Lanny, he wondered how old the guy was. Upon first glance, the man looked to be Jeff's age or a few years older, say forty, forty-two. But the eyes betrayed this when one got past the bearded face, the ancient soul that emanated from those chilling blue eyes. Lanny might be as young as twenty-four, twenty-five.

Lanny climbed inside the woodie, rubbing his arms against the chill.

Jeff smelled an amalgam, not altogether unpleasant, that reminded him of the market: iced-down fish, cured tobacco, fried-doughnut grease, garden loam, and vintage clothing.

"Talbot." Lanny nodded. "Ain't seen you around in awhile."

"You know how it is. Have to go farther and farther to scare up anything worthwhile."

"True enough."

"I've got a situation."

"Figured as much."

"Have I told you about my wife?"

"No, but figured there was one. You've been domesticated by somebody."

Jeff's smile was brief. "She's agoraphobic. You know much about that?"

"Enough."

Jeff looked at him, wide-eyed. He was always surprised to learn that people were basically familiar with agoraphobia. "When I got home tonight, she was gone."

Lanny nodded soberly. "Got a picture?"

Jeff took a photo from his wallet. "Her name's Sheila."

Lanny nodded again, and Jeff knew that the man would never repeat the story or forget the name. "Anything suspicious on the waterfront today? Anything at all, no matter how insignificant it might seem?"

"Nothing unusual in a criminal sense. Slim pickings, as far as old loot. Monday, you know." He paused for a second. "Almost bought me a fine-looking caduceus pin — twenties or thirties, I'd reckon — but the gal wearing it was . . . I don't know, distracted, nervous."

"Caduceus?" Jeff hadn't seen one of the medical symbols in some time, old or new. "Much of a market for those?"

"I've got a buyer who would've loved to get his hands on this one. Looked like sterling, with rhinestones down the shaft, sharp detail on the snakes and wings. I could've turned a good profit."

"Was she wearing it as a fashion statement, or do you think she was a doctor?"

"Nurse, actually. At least, she was dressed like one." Lanny smiled, settled back in the seat with a sigh. "Hot little thing. Long black hair, dark lips. Nothing like any nurse I've ever seen. Looked like Wonder Woman."

"You mean Lynda Carter?"

"Nah, the comic book character."

Jeff thought about the dozens of comic books inside the warehouse.

"Anyway," Lanny continued, "the guy driving the car kept trying to inch forward, like there was an inch to spare. You know what it's like, waiting in line to board the ferry. It was weird, like he was in a hurry, but I heard the gal say something that told me otherwise."

"Oh yeah?"

"Yeah. You see, she was smoking a cigarette, had her window cracked. She was complaining to the old man about taking one ferry just to get to another ferry to get to another place."

"That's strange. It's a pain to turn around if you've pulled up to the ticket booth and found out you're at the wrong pier, but it's better than going around the world."

"According to my way of thinkin', it is."

Something about the scenario didn't set right with Jeff. "I wonder if she was even a real nurse."

"She was more of a nurse than he was a driver. He almost ran over me when the line started moving."

"Did you get a look at him?"

"No. I'm sure it was a man, but I was on the wrong side to see his face."

"Maybe they were leftover tourists, not used to the ferry system."

"I thought so, too. Come to think of it, I glanced back at the plates. They were Washington."

"Rental, maybe."

"Not new enough. A Buick sedan, at least ten years old, I'd guess, with a maroon paint job that had seen better days."

Jeff pictured the dock scene Lanny had described, unsure why it raised a red flag. He chalked it up to training, the ingrained habit of noting anything out of the norm. Trouble was, those were usually the innocent ones. "So, you didn't get the pin?"

"Nah."

"Want something better?"

Lanny raised the photo of Sheila that he held firmly in his grasp. "Not without earning it."

"Call it a retainer."

Jeff hopped from the woodie, made a quick dash into the warehouse, and emerged with a stack of comic books. He handed them to Lanny.

Lanny whistled appreciatively. "Where did you find these?" Flipping through the pile of plastic-encased books, he said, "Mint, mostly, a few pristine mint. All from the Golden Age — that's thirties to fifties, in case you've got more." He shook his head, muttered "Unreal," then looked at Jeff. "Do you realize what you're giving away?"

Jeff shrugged. One had to pay well for information.

"You've got the contacts and the expertise for this sort of stuff." This "sort" meant comics, vinyl records, toys. "When I have more time, we can work out a split on the others I have."

"Sounds like you struck the mother lode."

"I haven't run an inventory yet, but it looks that way."

Lanny was obviously pleased with the gift. He pulled from the stack a copy of Our Flag Comics, dated 1941 with red, white, and blue letters indicative of Old Glory. "Wait a minute, you can't give me this. Don't you know that anything with a flag on it is primo right now?" He tried to hand it to

Jeff. "I can't accept it."

Jeff shook his head. "Sure you can. I've got two more from that year."

Lanny's mouth dropped.

"Just let me know if you hear anything."

"You've got it." Lanny opened the door, then hefted the stack of comics. "Thanks. The profit from these will carry me through next year."

"You've earned it."

"Not yet, but I'll try."

Maybe you already have, Jeff thought as his mind conjured up the vague image of a young nurse with a vintage caduceus and her invisible companion.

Jeff thought about calling Greer from the cellphone, then thought better of it. He didn't want to tie up the only two lines Sheila might try to call.

He made his way home, combing the streets as he drove for any sign of Sheila, anything out of the ordinary. Nothing. When he got back to the house, Greer met him at the door. But the look on the butler's face told him there was no news.

"I made a brief call to Mrs. Appleby, sir, as soon as you left. She contacted Miss Blessing, and Mr. Carver and his family. They're all here in the neighborhood, looking for the missus."

"Smart thinking, Greer. Thank you."

"You know Mrs. Appleby. She mentioned bringing in food. I told her it wasn't necessary, but I'm sure that when they are through searching, she'll go home and bake all night."

Jeff smiled, nodded. He understood the connotations of food — comfort, friendship, nurturing — and the therapy it could provide for anyone who liked to cook. Personally, his therapy was in antiques. He'd always lost himself in them, used them as an escape — even before he'd become a picker. Frequently, he had to instruct his wandering mind to get *back to people.*

It hadn't always been easy. But then Sheila had come along, come into his world and wrapped *life* around him like cashmere.

Perhaps, he surmised, food *was* Sheila. Sheila was his sustenance. He couldn't survive without her.

And as the world closed in on him, threatened to become too much for him to handle, he recognized the need for something to occupy his mind until Gordy arrived, or the cops called, or Sheila miraculously walked through the door.

Wearily, he climbed the service stairs to the third floor.

CHAPTER FIFTEEN

༄

Persons who meet the criteria as physically or mentally disabled, or a qualified veteran, may be eligible for a license at a reduced rate. These and other permanent physical disabilities may be qualifiers for a Designated Harvester Card, which allows another licensed person to assist a fisher with a disability in harvesting a daily limit of fish or shellfish.

— *Washington State Department of Fish and Wildlife*

Jeff opened the door that led into Sheila's antiques rooms, and his senses were assaulted by her fragrance, her presence, by *her*. He shivered, unsure whether it was from fear or cold, and stepped inside. Hugging himself, he held tight as if he might somehow control his nerves, prevent them from unraveling. He wasn't sure whether he could stand being in these rooms, but he didn't know where else to go.

The idea of sitting in the rooms he usually shared with his wife was unbearable. And, since they shared so much time together when he returned home every day, that left precious few segments of the large house in which he might seek respite, however fleeting it might be.

He couldn't face the dining room. Or the kitchen, for that matter. She was nearly always there when he came home from work, happily creating dinner. Whether it was one of her old favorites or some new and fabulous recipe she'd recently developed, she seemed most within her element while preparing food to nurture those she cared for. It wasn't lost on him that this task, this labor of love, did as much for her own well-being as it did for his.

He couldn't stay downstairs in the library. That realization hit him as soon as the police followed Greer out of the room earlier that evening. He and his wife often spent evenings there in front of a fire, either the both of them reading or Jeff researching antiques while Sheila cross-stitched or pored over cookbooks. The den was off-limits, too. When the couple wasn't in the library, they could usually be found in the large den, watching movies.

Forget the second floor. The lion's share of it was the master bedroom, *their* bedroom. He couldn't bring himself to go in there. Not without her.

The rest of the rooms on that story were used either as dressing rooms, or guest rooms rarely occupied. Jeff seldom visited any of those, other than the one that held his clothes and luggage.

Eliminating all those led him to the one area of the house where he believed he might grasp some sort of comfort. If any room was going to offer both an escape from reality and a sense that his wife was still with him, it was in the adjoining bedrooms on the third floor that his wife had converted into her own, private antiques store.

Sheila's presence in the room could be felt so strongly that Jeff allowed it to permeate his senses, to assure him that she was still alive out there somewhere, that she was unharmed. After allowing this sensation to soothe him, he embraced his next impression of the rooms, which was one of wonder.

He gazed at the antiques as he walked back and forth between the two rooms and recognized that his wife had created a phenomenal shopping oasis.

He noted, too, that she exhibited a bit of Blanche's keen eye for categorization. One room was full of things for the house, grouped according to tasks — cooking, reading, travel, writing, gardening, decorating — and he wondered whether this gave her a sense of categorizing her own space in what might be considered by some to be a small existence.

The second room resembled Vanessa Valentine's place. It was decidedly feminine, made more so by the ancient rosebud wallpaper that had been hung for Auntie Pim's nursery more than seventy years earlier. Auntie Pim's death suddenly felt more real to him than it had when she'd passed, shortly before he'd met Sheila. Primrose Talbot was his father's older sister, and she had raised Jeff, cared for him as if he were her own, after his parents had died in a boating accident off the Juan de Fucas.

In this room were antique dressmaker's forms decked out in Edwardian suits and confectionous hats; parasols with handles of sterling silver and horn and carved coral, both in umbrella stands and resting on chests of drawers; vintage dressing tables from the twenties, all loaded with gleaming dresser sets, scent bottles, costume jewelry.

He picked up an Art Nouveau mirror with

a lustrous silverplate that was part of a dresser set Sheila had recently mentioned purchasing.

Gripping the mirror's handle, he thought about Sheila's delicate hand holding it, too. He wanted to touch everything in the room, hold every piece that she had chosen for her future shopping trips. He wanted to absorb her, reach out to her. He wondered if she'd been in these rooms as recently as that afternoon.

He stood waiting, hoping that something, *anything*, would speak to him.

A bonnet caught his eye, and he reached for it, carefully lifting it from the nail upon which its tied bow was looped. It was red calico, dotted with little white and yellow daisies.

He tried to remember how long it had been since he'd found the bonnet for her. Three, four years? Sometimes, it was hard for him to understand how she could refrain from "buying" certain items from the store, when he knew he hadn't mistaken her excitement at first glance of the object. She practiced amazing restraint when it came to choosing from this massive collection of goods. It was a trait he only exhibited when dickering with a potential seller. But in his own home? No. He couldn't wait to display something new that he'd found for one of his collections.

A song from the seventies came to mind, one he'd sung to Sheila when he'd given her the bonnet:

"I'll give you a daisy a day, dear,
I'll give you a daisy a day.
I'll love you until all the rivers stand still,
And the four winds we know blow away."

Has Sheila ever worn this bonnet? He wondered. *Does she remember the song?* He breathed in its scent, trying to pick up his wife's fragrance, but he couldn't be sure, so surrounded was he by her things. He just wanted to hold her, comfort her, and be comforted *by* her. He untied the bow and, in a last-ditch effort to feel his wife's presence, placed the bonnet on his head. He checked his reflection in the looking glass. A part of him scorned the silliness, but he didn't care. Sheila loved it when he let go of macho inhibitions and embraced his playful side.

He wandered to the other room, chose a small, wrapped package from a shelf and smiled as he read the tag, which was written in his own hand: "For my darling Sheila, when you crave a new-old cuppa." He

269

looked up, chose another box. The tag on this one read: "For Sheila — something to chase away a rainy day." He gazed around the room, noted that over a dozen of the carefully wrapped presents were scattered about, perched on shelves or on recently polished pieces of furniture.

Sheila had hoarded so many things in the months before becoming completely house-bound. Some she'd wrapped herself, others she'd worked into artful displays, still others she'd purchased on-line after her agora-phobia had become so debilitating that she couldn't even go the few blocks over to Queen Anne Avenue to visit the little shops. Sometimes, she asked either Jeff or Greer to open those things she'd bought on-line, make sure they were in good shape, then wrap them for her to choose later from her rooms. They willingly accommodated.

Jeff was surprised that she'd hung on to ones that he'd specifically purchased for her. She had no clue what was waiting inside them, and it had been so long since he'd discovered them, that he couldn't recall the contents himself.

He felt a sudden urge to look inside one of the wrapped boxes. He toyed with this new compulsion, debated whether he would be crossing the bounds of privacy by doing so.

What could it hurt, he asked himself, if it provided some sort of connection to Sheila?

Package in hand, he darted through the passageway into the adjoining room where Sheila kept a small spinet desk stocked with office supplies. It was an Arts and Crafts desk, but he'd never been quite able to pinpoint either its maker or its value. Yet, he'd paid only fifty dollars for it at an estate sale and, sometimes, one had to be secure in the knowledge that monetary value wasn't everything. Besides, the desk had character. To either side of the slide-out writing surface was a curved cubbyhole, and all along the back were drawers and slots and shelves. The spinet part came from its design similar to an old piano whose ivories could be encased and locked for safekeeping.

Sheila kept the desk unlocked, as she often sat at it to write letters, plan menus, and keep records of catalog purchases.

Jeff opened little drawers until he found scissors, then sat at the desk and cut the pink satin ribbon with which the gift box was bound. He lifted the lid and unearthed a white teacup and saucer, decorated with gold trim and full-blown garnet roses. He remembered this set. He'd found it buried in a box he'd bought for practically nothing at an estate sale.

The cup wasn't very valuable as cup and saucer sets go, but it matched a set that his wife was slowly amassing for the dining room. She was so into dishes that she'd set about completing a different service for each of the four seasons.

Jeff swallowed against the lump in his throat as he realized that she hadn't seen this one.

He needed a diversion and, after casting about, settled on the doors under the window seat. He opened the doors and discovered several Dobbs hatboxes. The black and yellow boxes from the Fifth Avenue hatter got the best of his curiosity. He pried a lid off one and peered inside. A sheet of copy paper on the top read: SAVE FOR JEFF'S CHRISTMAS.

He reddened, as if he'd been caught peeking through a window. Trembling, he started to replace the lid. He stopped. These were items Sheila had tracked down for him, stowed away until that time when the calendar announced that December had arrived, and the couple would exchange a gift every few days throughout the month.

Perhaps, if he looked at the items, he could feel Sheila's presence, fill a small portion of the enormous void that was growing inside him like a cancer.

The first item was a collapsible top hat of black silk, in pristine condition. Its label read: MADE IN WEST GERMANY, and stickers indicated that it was "long oval" in size $7^3/8$. His size. He marveled at Sheila's ability to track down the perfect gifts.

Next, he withdrew a small navy blue case with the name of a jeweler stamped across it in gold. He pried open the hinged lid and found an exquisite pair of baton-shaped onyx cuff links — nineteen-twenties French, if he wasn't mistaken — with a garnet cabochon at either end encircled by diamonds. Marlene Dietrich wore a similar pair, he seemed to recall, and the thought crossed his mind that these might actually have belonged to the screen legend.

He shuffled through the rest of the hat box, hoping to find a letter of provenance that would tell him whether the cuff links had a fascinating history, but he found nothing. Well, he thought, maybe Sheila had stored the letter in a folder.

Sheila.

The thought of her snapped him back to the present. He glanced at his watch, realized that less than three minutes had passed since he'd last checked the time. He'd become so lost in the comfort of the antiques, that he had allowed nearly three minutes to pass without thinking about the current situation, the realization that Sheila was out there somewhere — alone, disoriented, hurt.

Guilt washed over him. Hastily, he put the gifts back into the box, finishing just as Greer tapped on the door.

Jeff looked up, detected a brief and almost imperceptible expression of astonishment on his butler's face, and remembered that he was still wearing the bonnet.

Greer was holding a large silver tray. "Sir, you should have some dinner."

"Thanks, but I'm not hungry." Jeff pulled the bonnet from his head. "I thought I could feel her presence. I thought she would walk in and ask me what I was up to, ferreting out Christmas packages like a ten-year-old. But . . . I feel helpless here."

"With all due respect, sir, you should eat something. When the missus returns home, it's going to take both of us to care for her. We must take care of ourselves until then."

Jeff looked at the tray of food, shook his head.

Greer set the tray on the desk, poured water from a silver pitcher over the ice in a glass. The cubes cracked loudly in the silence, setting Jeff's nerves on edge and causing the hairs on his arms to stand out.

Greer quietly left the room.

Jeff checked his watch. Gordy should be arriving soon. And the cops should have called by now. And none of this should be happening but it was.

He picked up the tray, walked down the service stairs to the kitchen, found Greer making a seemingly heartless attempt at eating his own dinner.

The butler rose and took the tray.

"May I join you, Greer? I'd rather not eat alone tonight."

"Of course, sir." Greer quickly arranged a proper place setting on the table for his employer.

They ate out of duty and in silence. Both men jumped at every sound, no matter how insignificant, that came from the house, the street, the neighborhood.

The doorbell rang and they shot to their feet and ran to the front door. Jeff paused an instant, as the possibility of bad news hit him. He stepped back a foot as Greer opened the door.

Apart from Sheila, there was no one Jeff would've wanted to have seen more than Gordon Easthope.

Gordy was as big and solid as a Wooten desk at six-foot-four and weighing two-eighty if he weighed a pound. He was dressed all in gray from his suit to his overcoat to his snap-brim fedora and he looked as if he'd stepped straight out of a Dick Tracy strip.

In a voice with the bite and warmth of whiskey, he said: "Let's bring our little girl home."

PART THREE

THE CATCH

ॐ

El pez muere por la boca.
(The fish dies because
he opens his mouth.)
— *Spanish Proverb, Anonymous*

CHAPTER SIXTEEN

≈

I love such mirth as does not make
friends ashamed to look upon one another next morning.
— Izaak Walton
The Compleat Angler,
1653–1655

"You know the drill." Gordy appeared calm
and collected on the outside. Inside, however, Jeff knew that his mentor's wheels were
grinding against themselves at a frantic rate.

Jeff provided a thumbnail sketch for
Gordy and a Seattle bureau agent by the
name of Simms (who looked too young to
shave), beginning with his arrival home and
ending with his waterfront visit to Lanny.

When he finished, Gordy skimmed the
notes he'd been making. "Are you sure
you've given me all of it, right down to

smoothing your hangnails?"

"That's it, Gordy."

"So, no lights *anywhere?*"

"Other than the computer screen? No."

"Did the cops go through the house, after your initial search?"

"No."

Gordy shook his head, studied his scribbles. "The door. You said it *pushed* open."

"Right. It's tricky. You have to give it an extra push for it to click. We've got a repairman coming to take a look at it . . . ?" He looked at Greer with the question.

"Tomorrow, sir."

Gordy said, "Listen to yourself, Jeff. You're thinking as if Sheila was *in* the house when the door was closed. Try it the other way. What if someone was in here, wanted to make it look like she'd left on her own? He pulled the door shut, but didn't know about the tricky latch."

"Damn it, Gordy, you're right." Jeff rubbed a hand across his face. "I'm too torn up to look at this through the eyes of an investigator."

"Don't beat yourself up for that. Emotions outweigh training. Why do you think they prefer agents who are unencumbered?"

Gordy turned to Simms. "Got your print kit on you?"

The agent nodded.

"Let's check her office then."

Jeff led the way up to the third floor.

"We're definitely dealing with someone who knows what he's doing," Gordy said after they'd dusted for prints. "It's too clean. Not even the hint of a smudge from her hand on the mouse."

"We've got prints on the phone, though," said Simms. "Probably hers."

"So," Jeff said, "whoever was here touched the computer but nothing else."

"Looks that way, and since no other lights were on in the house, we can assume it was before dusk.

"By now," Gordy continued, "I'm sure you've run through a mental list of people you arrested. Anyone you dealt with in the past who might have gotten out recently?"

"I'd thought of that, but I don't think so. Besides, the people I put away are thieves, not killers. They'd be more likely to kill in order to get their hands on an antique than for getting caught stealing one."

The screen saver popped up on the monitor. Gordy appeared to be studying the lighthouse's beacon. "Jeff, do *you* ever use this computer? Any files in here that somebody might've been after?"

Jeff felt a vise tighten around his chest. He sat down at the computer, double-clicked an icon on the desktop. "Saturday, I forwarded some of Bill's links to Sheila's E-mail address. I checked last night to make sure I had done it right. They were here."

Bill. Jeff realized that Gordy didn't know about the murder. He told his ex-partner what he knew. Gordy was shocked and saddened, but the special agent in him kicked in and he asked the questions that needed answers. Jeff supplied them mechanically.

He turned back to the computer and checked the E-mail program's Inbox. The files weren't there. He began double-clicking folders listed in a column on the screen's left side, opening each one to see if Sheila had assigned the links to a separate folder.

Nothing.

The vise tightened further. "They're not here."

"Check the trash."

Jeff opened the Recycle Bin. It was empty. Fear overtook him as he realized the danger Sheila was in.

Quickly, he told Gordy the rest of the story, explained how the sheriff had asked him to check Bill's fishing links against some of the items he was going to sell for Mrs. Rhodes. He reminded Gordy about the antique lures that had been stolen from Bill earlier, and how the links had indicated that Bill was tracking down and purchasing those stolen lures.

When Jeff had finished, Gordy said, "It ties together somehow."

"Yeah, but how?"

"Where did you say the lures are? The ones you're supposed to sell?"

"I've got them in storage, in a warehouse down on the waterfront."

"Who knew about the forwarded links?"

Jeff thought it over. "Just about everybody I saw over the weekend. But . . . it doesn't make sense. Everything points to Bill's widow as his killer."

"Which probably means that she didn't do it. I wonder if the sheriff over there knows whether Bill had a pre-nup. If he didn't, then the wife wouldn't have had a motive. She could've taken him to the cleaners in divorce court." Gordy's brow wrinkled. "Is Bill's computer at the bait shop or the house?"

"House."

"We need to know who's behind the sale of those stolen lures. Call up your sheriff. Have her check Bill's computer."

Jeff thought about the sheriff's ignorance regarding computers. She was smart, though, smarter than a lot of people seemed to give her credit for. She would recruit some techno junkie from her staff to go with her to the Rhodes house. He used Greer's cellphone, punched in the sheriff's number. As he did so, he said to Gordy, "You know, I was down at the warehouse a couple of hours ago, but I wasn't looking for anything suspicious. I'm not sure whether the lures were still there or not."

"You go to the warehouse, see if it's secure. I'll alert our Internet team, get 'em ready to hit warp speed when you get something from those links. We can pick up a trail, track down who's selling the stolen goods, see if it gives us what we need to find Sheila. Simms, you get this Sergeant Wyatt on the horn, see if the locals have turned up anything." Gordy stabbed at the keypads on his own cellphone, then put a hand on Jeff's arm. "And take a gun, you hear me?"

Jeff nodded, pressed Send on the cell, and started toward the library.

Gordy put the phone to his ear. "We'll need some maps of the neighborhood. Ferry schedules, too."

Greer said, "I'll see to it, sir," and hurried from the room.

★ ★ ★

"McIvers here."

Her voice sounded tired. When Jeff spoke, his sounded more so. "Sheriff? Jeff Talbot again."

"If you're calling about the Black Widow, she's clean. Matter of fact, she took a call from Bill while she was at the beauty shop, probably no more than an hour before he was murdered. My deputy's mother said that Tanya was there all afternoon."

"That means there's still a killer out there somewhere. A killer who may have my wife."

Silence. Then, "What did you say?"

"You heard right." Jeff went on to explain Sheila's disappearance, the missing computer links, and — although he wasn't sure why — he threw in the part about the couple Lanny had overheard.

When he was through, the sheriff said, "I'll swing by the office and grab Manning. He stays up on all this new technology. It won't hurt to keep an eye out for that maroon car, either. Jeff?" She paused. "Has it crossed your mind that all this might be tied together?"

"That's what Gordy said, too, and it scares the hell out of me. Another thing that scares me is the fact that I can't find the missing link." Actually, there were *two* missing links — the one that connected Sheila's disappearance to this whole mess, and the one that might hook together the scam to sell Bill's stolen lures, thus leading to whoever was behind all of this.

He thought for a moment. "Sheriff, I'm headed to the warehouse now to make sure Bill's lures are still there. After that, I'm coming back to the village. If there *is* a connection, then I'm just as likely to get a lead on Sheila over there as I am here. And the cops over here just want me to stay out of the way."

"Better hurry. Last ferry will be pulling out soon."

"Thanks." Jeff punched End, then dropped the phone into his shirt pocket. Next, he moved two volumes on collecting Old West firearms and retrieved his weapon.

The gun felt cold and strange in his palm. He'd rarely used it, even when he was working undercover. It crossed his mind that he may not even be able to handle it anymore. But when he thought about Sheila and the chance that she'd been abducted by Bill's killer, he knew that he could, and would, do whatever it took to bring her home safely. He grabbed a clip from the drawer in his library desk, threw on his windbreaker, and ran to the car.

For the third time that day, he drove down to the waterfront.

He clasped the automatic tightly in his right hand, surprised that his palm was clammy. Had he lost his nerve in the years since working law enforcement? He didn't think so, but he was irritated that even the possibility required conscious thought. He racked a shell into the chamber, then got out of the car.

The service door of the warehouse creaked slightly as Jeff pulled it open. The skin crawled at the back of his neck. He had dashed in here not two hours earlier, giving no thought to the fact that it might hold danger or leads or anything else, other than the benign acquisitions from an old lady's odd existence and a dead man's collection of fishing lures. Now, his senses were at top alert.

He flipped the light switch, gave the room a fast once-over, then walked to the back where he'd left the boxes of Bill's lures.

They were there, with everything intact. He wondered then whether Sheila's abductor had gone through their home, searching for the collection. He tried to recall whether he'd mentioned the warehouse to anyone, but he wasn't sure. If not, then only Sheila, Greer, and Blanche knew that he was using it. Oh, and the movers. Two pairs of movers, actually. He knew that Blanche wouldn't hire anyone who didn't pass scrutiny. He also knew that the more people who were in on a secret, the more chances there were for double-cross.

He shook his head against all the images. *Don't get paranoid. Keep your eye on the ball and not on the game.*

He looked at the cellphone's screen, concerned that, somehow, he'd missed an incoming call. But the display gave no indication that he had. It did show him the time, an ominous 11:48. The thought of the calendar turning to another date while Sheila was unaccounted for bumped his panic level up a notch.

He locked up and climbed back into the woodie. As he drove north, he debated whether his decision to return to the fishing village was a wise one. What if he did, and Sheila was still in Seattle? But what if he didn't, and she was over there, across the water.

He replayed every piece of information that had been revealed, no matter how trivial it had seemed at the time. He went over conversations and sorted through snatches of dialogues. He envisioned computer screens he'd seen over the last several days, tried to remember what he'd seen on which monitor, what he'd heard from which speakers, who had been present. Images flashed across his mind like flickering frames from silent-movie reels — people, lures, odors, sounds, fish, dolls, scents, waders, spears, roads. He went over questions and answers, and questions without answers.

That's when it hit him. A constant. Something with a common denominator, if only he could remember . . . He couldn't get it to click into place, but he knew that he had to go back.

The answers lay somewhere in the sleepy little community across the water.

CHAPTER SEVENTEEN

᠅

Bait the hook well: this fish will bite.
— Shakespeare
Much Ado about Nothing

The town was laced up tight as a Victorian corset when Jeff slowed at the only traffic light in the community. He took advantage of the minute between red and green to punch in the sheriff's cellphone number. Had anyone told him a week earlier that he would soon, and suddenly, come to rely on cellphones, he would have laughed in his face.

He hit Send and waited.

"Yeah?" McIvers answered, not wasting any time.

"It's me. I'm here, working my way north."

"Take it easy. This fog's moving in fast."

"Right. Did you get hold of Tanya Rhodes?"

"Afraid not. I've called, driven out there, checked with just about everybody I know. Finally found out she's on a nip-and-tuck holiday, won't be home till Sunday. Gave her maid the week off."

"We may not need her. Can you meet me at Coop's?"

"Sure. Matter of fact, I'm pulling in now."

"I see you," he said, then added, "The science of cellular technology." He punched End, pulled in behind the sheriff's cruiser.

The parking lot was empty, except for a black pickup in front of the door. The sheriff pulled in beside it, and Jeff parked next to her.

"Coop's truck," the sheriff said. "He's probably staying the night. Does that as often as not."

"Lucky for us."

The sheriff tried the door, discovered that it was locked, then pounded on it.

"Hang on," a voice bellowed from inside.

Coop swung the door open, greeted the two with a double-barrel shotgun.

Instinct made Jeff reach for his pocket, then stop.

"Coop, put that damned thing away before I do it for you." The sheriff stepped around him and into the bar. "We need to pick your brain."

"Can't it wait till tomorrow? I've gotta get the cash drawer to balance, then get some shut-eye. Monday night football wears me out."

Jeff stepped inside. "It'll just take a minute."

Coop glanced at the sheriff, who was already perched on one of the barstools. "Like I could stop *that* gal, God love her." He closed the door. "Got some coffee left over, if you want it."

"Sounds good," Jeff said.

As Coop poured, Jeff got the conversation rolling. "Vanessa Valentine told me that she and Bill were here a few weeks ago. He was showing her how to use the Internet on your computer?"

Coop chuckled. "Yeah. I doubt it stuck, though. Val's never been one for technology."

Jeff smiled. "She told me that, too. But she did say that Bill shot out of here in a hurry. Do you know why?"

"Can't say as I do. I just figured he and Val had had a fallin' out." He raised a brow. "Know what I mean?"

Jeff nodded. "So, neither of them said anything about it later?"

"Nope. To tell you the truth, I'd forgotten all about it till you mentioned it. I'd even intended to check on that auction, see what happened with it. But things got busy, then Bill got killed, and —"

"What do you mean, 'auction?' " Jeff leaned forward.

"You know, on-line auction. I was curious. At least I thought I was, but since I never got back to it . . ." He shrugged. "I guess I figured it could wait. Anyhow, Bill had left in such a hurry that he didn't log off. When I went back to disconnect, there was this auction page on the —"

"How were you going to check back on it?" Jeff set his cup down. "Did you make a note of the Web site?"

"You don't know much about story-telling, do you, son?"

"Sorry, Coop," the sheriff interjected, "but this could be important."

Coop's interest level appeared to go up. "Do you think it's got something to do with Bill's murder?"

"Chance of it," the sheriff said. "Looks like somebody's got a theft ring going. Talbot's wife has been abducted," she added, nodding toward Jeff. "We're trying to see if it's all interconnected."

"Why didn't you say so?" Coop loped to the back, Jeff and the sheriff at his heels. "I bookmarked the damn thing."

The office wasn't much, a windowless cubbyhole with cheap paneling and a strip of track lighting on the ceiling. Coop took a seat in a squeaky chair in front of the computer screen, punched a key to connect. When it did, he scrolled through the Favorites list until he found the link. He clicked it and waited.

The screen that popped up had the bright eBay logo at the top. An inch or so below that was a sentence typed in red letters which read, *This auction has ended.* Coop scrolled down until he came to the image of a lure. To its right was a paragraph giving a detailed description. Above it, in red block letters, was the name. It read: The Weedless Widow.

The sheriff pulled a folded sheaf of papers from her jacket pocket, flattened them on the desk, and flipped to the last page. Jeff recognized the pages as Bill's inventory list. "Bill was a stickler for organization, so these are in alphabetical order . . . here it is!" She stabbed the paper. "Says 'Heddon, 1928, bullfrog, buck-tail conceals single hook, two steel wires extend over back to provide weedless feature.' "

She leaned closer to the computer screen and added, "Notice anything different about this one and your typical finds, Talbot?"

"Yeah. The same thing I found on all the buck-tail lures in Bill's collection." Jeff tapped the screen. "His identifier. The red thread hidden in the center of the buck's tail."

"Coop," Jeff grabbed a notepad and pen, "what does the site tell us about the seller?"

Coop maneuvered the mouse, moved to the top of the page. "Says here that he's in the Washington region. He's got a new screen name, too. See these?" Coop used the cursor to point out a pair of dark glasses next to the nickname. "These shades mean it's a new nickname, hasn't been using it for more than thirty days."

"Keep the screen where it is while I call in with this information." Jeff punched Gordy's number. When he answered, Jeff read off the pertinent information.

"Now we're cookin' with gas," Gordy said after he'd verified the facts. "I'll call you back."

Jeff and the sheriff thanked Coop and went out to lean against the cruiser in the parking lot.

"Has anything developed over here since we spoke this afternoon?"

"Yeah, actually. Remember that species that Raven said lasts only ten minutes or so out of water?"

"Pacu, wasn't it? Or, was it pleco?"

"Pacu. The plecos can last, like, an hour. Anyway, I've been going over there to feed the survivors. When I went tonight, I saw a pacu in the tank. Must've been hiding behind something before."

Jeff considered this new information. "So, the murderer could have left as little as a few minutes before we got there?"

"Sounds like it."

The fog had thickened and they stood silently for a moment, listening to the night sounds that seemed magnified by the thick haze.

"This will be one for the record," the sheriff said. "The murderer was caught by a fish."

Jeff rubbed his eyes. "This is killing me, Sheriff. Not knowing where she is, but knowing that there's a lead here somewhere and I can't get it to click. Now Sheila's been dragged into it, and I'm letting her down. If they hurt her, I . . . I don't know how I'll deal with it."

"Try to hang tight. You've got a lot of people working on it, right?"

"I suppose so. I mean, there are friends, and cops, and friends who *are* cops — FBI, anyway. We've all made phone calls, pulled strings . . ."

Phone calls. Was there something about a phone call? He played the last five days over and over in his mind, casting about for the elusive *something* that fluttered there. He chased after it, tried to snag it. And just as he cornered the thing, his cellphone rang.

He jumped, practically knocking the sheriff off her feet, and fumbled the phone out of the shirt pocket located over his pounding heart. He punched a button.

"Talbot."

"Jeff, it's Gordy." He sounded out of breath. "We tracked down the guy from the Web page, sent a good cop–bad cop team to his place south of Tacoma. Didn't take long for him to give them the name of a corporation he was working for. I've pulled more strings than a puppeteer, but the upshot is that I've got a certain investor's name. Jeff, you're not going to believe who it is."

"Try me."

Gordy spit out names, dates, statistics, as if he were writing up one of his infamous shorthand lists. Jeff knew the codes. He'd been trained by Gordon Easthope, had learned from him, and retained all he had learned.

Gordy's information confirmed Jeff's suspicions. It had finally come together in his brain. The common denominator was nothing more than a sound, a sound that had been eating at his thoughts, a sound that, when it had traveled over the phone wires, was at once familiar yet totally out of place.

Jeff opened the driver's door of the cruiser. The sheriff caught up to speed quick and hopped behind the wheel. Jeff rode shotgun, told her where to head, then finished the conversation with Gordy. "You call the state, tell 'em where to find us."

"Got it. And, Jeff? Be careful. Don't let him present a case that will muddle your good senses."

"Don't worry."

As the sheriff drove down the long stretch of highway, straining to see through the dense fog that had moved in, Jeff pieced together a scenario, a working hypothesis, so that he might plan his approach.

Likely, the abductor had gone to the Talbot house with the hope of sweet-talking Sheila, had used some excuse in order to see the links Jeff had forwarded, had told her that he was playing a role in the investigation and needed to verify the on-line information.

But something had gone wrong, and Sheila had been forced to go with the deceiver. Jeff hoped the person had done this only as a way to buy some time while he determined what his recourses were, to throw Jeff off a trail that Jeff himself hadn't realized he was on.

It was beginning to make sense. The mysterious woman wearing a caduceus. A nurse. Someone had thought ahead, had known that Sheila wouldn't leave without a struggle. Therefore, he had gone prepared to sedate her, erase the files, use what was likely the nurse's maroon Buick rather than one of his own vehicles, and abduct Sheila for as long as it took to wipe out the technological trail that led to him.

Only he had missed one thing. He hadn't known about Vanessa Valentine's computer lesson at Coop's Tavern. If he had, both Coop and Val would have been in danger as well.

He filled the sheriff in on Gordy's report and his own thoughts, then laid out his plan. It was the only approach that might prevent their suspect from panicking.

As the sheriff drove along the empty highway, Jeff reached in his jacket pocket, verified that a small yet significant item was still there. It was the one thing that might mean all the difference between success and failure. It was the key to unlocking the mystery, and he'd had it with him all along.

CHAPTER EIGHTEEN

People who fish keep secrets.
People who gamble tell lies.
People with something to hide from their
peers
Are dressed up in Satan's disguise.
— Jeff Talbot

He instructed the sheriff to park the cruiser on the shoulder of the highway. The fog was heavier now, had fallen over the area like a net. Concerned that they might not maintain a sense of direction, he grabbed the sheriff's hand, gave it a quick squeeze, and held on to it as they made their way blindly down the lane.

They were almost upon the cabin when they caught first glimpse of a dim shaft of light cutting its way through the fog, reaching for the pine needles that carpeted the ground in front of the porch. It was coming from the window off the dining room, and Jeff recalled seeing that same light four nights earlier as he returned from his first visit to Bill Rhodes's home. It emanated from the lamp that typically served as the night-light.

The sheriff tapped his arm, then pointed at the corner of the house. He could barely make out the fender of a vehicle. It looked maroon.

Stealthily, the pair climbed the steps and crept across the porch to the front door. A board creaked quietly under Jeff's foot, and he cursed silently. He motioned the sheriff to one side of the doorway, while he took position on the other side. They waited. No noise came from within, yet an unmistakable sound on the porch convinced Jeff that his puzzle pieces fit. As he slid his key into the hole on the knob's back plate, a cricket chirped in the silence, his song reverberating in the still night.

It might have been the same one Jeff had heard over a cellphone, a hundred years ago a phone that he had thought was in downtown Seattle. It was funny what you heard and didn't pay attention to.

He prayed that the tumblers clicking into place wouldn't echo as the cricket's song had. He moved in slow motion, unlocked the door, steadily, carefully, turned the knob.

Simultaneously, he pushed the door open and reached for his weapon. Stepping through the narrow opening, he scanned the dining area, the kitchen, and the half of the living room visible to him. He pivoted to secure the rest of the room and found himself staring into the feral eyes of Judge Richard Larrabee.

"Put the gun on the table," the Judge ordered.

Jeff ignored him. "Where is she?" He started toward the hallway.

The Judge waved the gun.

Jeff stopped. "She'd better be okay, or I swear, Judge, I'll kill you where you stand."

"She's fine. I had no intention of hurting her. But if you kill me, the person guarding your wife will kill her. Don't doubt me on that." He steadied his aim. "The table. Now. And empty your pockets while you're at it."

Jeff's training told him not to relinquish his weapon, and in a rush he understood why you didn't get involved when a loved one's life was at stake. It helped him to know that the sheriff was outside, and that she undoubtedly had put a plan into the works. Finally, he followed the Judge's instruction, regret consuming him as he laid the gun among his personal effects.

"I underestimated you, Jeff. How did you find me?"

"Let me see her."

"You will, in due time. But first, I need to make sure you understand why she's here. I had to prove that your picture-perfect life isn't as neat and tidy as you thought it was. Your wife isn't as safe and sound behind those walls as you've fooled yourself into believing. Do you *see* that you're not immune to the outside world? Do you *realize* that I — or anyone else, for that matter — can come into your so-called haven and take from you what matters most?

"You have a choice," he continued. "You can either do as I say, and forget everything you know about Bill's lures, or you can become as paranoid as your wife. Just back off, stop pursuing those Internet sales, and you and I can go back to business as usual." He shrugged, smiled. "You see? It's as simple as that. If you don't, then I'll have to come back for your wife. You'll never have any peace, always worrying about what's going to happen to her. Now, really, Jeff, is her life worth a few stolen lures?"

"Was Bill's?"

The Judge's face registered regret. "He called me Wednesday, said he'd tracked down a company that was selling his stolen lures. He'd even come up with several screen names in order to bid on his lures and find out who was shipping them. I told him to sit tight, that I'd take a look at what he had when I arrived for the weekend.

"When I got to the bait shop, Bill had been doing his homework. He named the company — the company *I* had invested in — and I knew it was only a matter of time before he pieced things together." The Judge wiped sweat from his upper lip with the back of his hand. "I thought I could fix it. I swear to you, I never intended to kill him."

Jeff needed to steer the conversation away from the murder, try to keep the Judge from hitting the panic button again. "Why did you do this to Sheila?"

The Judge appeared to regain his composure. "I doubt she'll remember what's happened. I told the nurse to use a strong sedative. Bringing Sheila over here was nothing more than an insurance policy, a means of getting you to back off. It's worth it, isn't it? You leave me alone, and I'll leave her alone." He laughed nervously. "Don't make me have to go through this again, Jeff.

But know that I will if I have to. And, I assure you, it's not that difficult to find a woman who *never* leaves her house."

The Judge leaned against the rocks of the fireplace. "Don't forget who you called when you needed help tonight. Your old buddy, Judge Larrabee.

"Sure," he went on, "the cops told you they would look for her. Do you want to know why? I told them, 'Humor him, guys. He's an old friend who's not home all that much, if you get my drift.' Not a lie, is it Jeff?"

Jeff's heart pounded against his chest wall as he fought to maintain control.

"Bill's widow was a hell of a lot easier to deal with than your wife. She didn't ask for proof, or question my involvement in the case. She didn't even stay in the basement with me after she pointed out the computer. But Sheila? Too smart. Watched me like a hawk. Asked too many questions.

"Of course," he continued, "you know by now that I don't have to worry about the files on your computer." He stabbed his finger as if he were striking a keyboard. "Gone. All of them.

"You're my only remaining worry. Or, rather, you *were*. Now that you know I can get to Sheila anytime I want, you'll go along with my plan."

"Do you have any idea what your *plan* has done to my wife?"

The Judge looked surprised. "Do *you* have any idea what I've gone through to get my campaign off the ground? You don't know what something like this costs. When I first invested in Internet sales, I didn't know we'd be selling stolen property." He waved his hands. Jeff kept his eyes on the gun. "I know, I know," the Judge said. "I should've asked questions. But, c'mon. Nobody asks questions that they don't want the answers to. In less than eight weeks, I had more than enough to run my campaign! I sure as *hell* wasn't going to ask questions at that point.

"No one would've gotten hurt if Bill hadn't been so damned stubborn. I tried to reason with him, offered to replace the lures if he'd just look the other way. He wouldn't listen. I offered money — lots of money. He didn't want it. Next thing I knew, he was lunging at me. I . . . I'm not sure what happened after that. I remember thinking that one minute he was about to accept my offer, and the next minute, he was on the floor."

The Judge seemed to be in a fog. After a moment, he emerged clear-eyed. "Hell, he thought his lures were worth so damn much. Their value wasn't a patch on what I had invested in that company. How could he put their value above something as noble as leadership and the promise of a better life?

"Oh, well. That's behind us now. I feel bad about it, but I'm not going to let it get in the way of my goals. I didn't go there to kill him, but I couldn't let his attitude change the course of everything."

"It did, though, didn't it, Judge?" The sheriff's voice echoed from down the hall.

The Judge wheeled.

Colleen McIvers stood in the hallway, a thirty-eight aimed at Larrabee's chest.

Jeff smiled in spite of himself. The Judge had been so intent upon protecting himself, so keen on justifying his actions, that he hadn't thought to do one simple thing: remove Jeff's key from the front door. Apparently, the sheriff had slipped the key from the hole and used it to come in through the back.

"Talbot." The Judge backed up enough to put both Jeff and the sheriff in his line of vision. "Tell her how this is going down, or you and your wife will never sleep with your eyes closed again."

"Did you see her, Sheriff? Is she okay?"

"She's been sedated, but she's going to be fine. That nurse, though . . ."

"What did you do?" the Judge asked.

"I gave her a dose of her own medicine." The sheriff didn't crack a smile.

It was all Jeff could do to keep from running to the back of the house. For the moment, though, he needed to see things through here, try to help keep the Judge calm. If the man panicked and started shooting, everybody would lose.

"You're all out of options, Judge," the sheriff said. "Nothing left to gamble with."

"You're not going to shoot me, Sheriff." His voice had taken on a condescending tone. "Why don't you just go on back to the station? Tell her, Jeff. This is between you and me." The Judge's arm faltered, the gun wavered slightly.

Jeff glanced at the sheriff. He'd never seen a steadier aim. If the Judge had any brains at all, he wouldn't underestimate this woman. She was in her element, unlike Sheila. The Judge had used Sheila's weakness to control her, but if he thought that the sheriff had a weakness, he was going to be surprised.

"Put the gun down, Judge."

"I can't do that, Sheriff."

"Don't force my hand."

"Do you honestly think you can shoot me? You don't have it in you."

Jeff intervened, tried another tact. "Let me call Kyle for you, Judge. Just talk to him, okay?"

"I told you. This has to stay between you and me."

The sheriff said, "It's already way beyond that, Judge. Now put down the gun."

"That's something that I'm not willing to do."

"I'm telling you for the last time. You either get on with it, or you get it over with. It's your call."

Jeff had been in that place where the sheriff now stood, had realized that the situation was going south, had wondered whether he would be the one to pull the trigger or the one to fall. Cornered animals felt trapped, and that feeling blinded them beyond all reason.

A cornered person usually panicked, lost his focus, let his eyes dart, watching, guessing, second-guessing. Jeff saw only the profiles of both the Judge and the sheriff as they faced each other, but it was enough to tell him who was the professional.

Keep your eye on the ball and not on the game. Gordy had said it to him a thousand times, drilled it into his memory for life. Earlier he had consciously reminded himself of it. Now, he could see that someone along the way had made sure the sheriff knew it, too.

The silence in the room pounded against his eardrums, built to a deafening ring. His gaze darted between the two people before him and in the second of time that followed, he saw a slight flicker of the Judge's eye, a twitch of a muscle in his arm, the expression on his face change from surprise to panic to wild defiance.

He saw the sheriff, face unchanged, eyes locked on Larrabee, and he watched her squeeze the trigger an instant before the Judge did the same. The Judge fell, and his shot went wild. The bullet struck a window. Glass shattered and rained onto the porch.

The ringing magnified. Smoke stung Jeff's eyes as he fought to take in the scene.

Sheriff McIvers kept the gun sighted in on the Judge, now lying still on the floor. She blinked rapidly against the smoke. To Jeff, she said, "Go get your wife."

CHAPTER NINETEEN

ॐ

HOW TO RELEASE FISH: When you need to release a fish there are some special precautions you can take to give it a good chance of surviving . . . If you've removed the fish from the water, get it back in as soon as possible.

— *Washington State Department of Fish and Wildlife*

Sheila was lying on the bed, struggling against a fog of sedation. She wore a T-shirt that read: FISHERMEN ARE BORN HONEST BUT THEY GET OVER IT.

Jeff saw an ironic joke in the statement and would have commented on it had the glazed eyes staring at him given any indication that his wife was behind them.

He located the sweater set and slacks that Greer had described earlier for the police.

He carefully removed the sweat-soaked T-shirt and dressed his wife in her own clothes, believing that every effort toward normalcy was one step closer to having his wife back.

He held her, spoke softly to her as the medicinal fog lifted.

The approaching sirens seemed vague and distant. After a few moments, Sheriff McIvers came to the bedroom. "Do you want her taken to the hospital?"

"No, thanks. The quicker I get her home to her own surroundings, the better off she'll be. I'll have Greer call Sheila's regular doctor, have him come to the house."

The sheriff nodded. "Why don't you move her to one of the other rooms for now, while we get Sleeping Beauty wheeled out?"

He nodded. "Are you okay, Sheriff?"

"I'm never okay when I have to kill somebody. But when they panic? It's all in the body language, you know."

"I know." He cradled his wife in his arms, started toward the door, then stopped and turned back. "Thanks, Sheriff."

She looked surprised. "You would've done the same for me."

They were driving up Queen Anne

Avenue with only a few blocks left to travel when the sedative lost its hold and Sheila realized she wasn't home.

Wide-eyed, she gripped the armrest with one hand and Jeff's hand with the other and pushed with her feet against the floorboard, as if she could bury herself in the confines of the car.

She gulped air repeatedly, then began hyperventilating as Jeff brought the woodie to a stop in their driveway.

He rooted around in the car and found a paper bag that still held doughnuts he'd purchased at the market earlier in the day. He dumped them out, then forced his wife to breathe into the bag.

As her breathing returned to normal — or as near as it could, for someone who was frightened nearly out of her mind — Jeff was grateful for the dark. He couldn't imagine her reaction had she been able to see clearly the openness that surrounded her.

It took him an hour to get Sheila from the car to the house. Apparently, something inside her had accepted the car's interior as her new surroundings — a sort of coping mechanism, he presumed, that had kicked in as a way of preventing a complete breakdown.

He pointed out to her that every light in

the house was on, asked her to trust him to get her inside safely. He ended up prying her fingers loose from the dash, speaking to her as he would a child, promising her she would never be left alone again. He wrapped her in a blanket and carried her inside.

The house was empty, except for Greer. Jeff had called ahead, told Greer and Gordy that Sheila had been located, warned them what to expect. He was told that several friends were at the house, having drifted in from the streets and their search: Blanche and Trudy, Sam and Helen Carver and three of their five daughters, all of whom had brought significant others.

Greer had sounded animated over the phone, his obvious relief and excitement almost getting the better of his strict training. He assured Jeff that he would inform everyone of Mrs. Talbot's safety, then would clear the house of people so that Sheila wouldn't have the added trauma of a house full of well-meaning, but anxious guests.

Now, the butler reached out and touched Sheila's arm, as if to reassure himself that it was really her. The simple gesture caused tears to well up in Jeff's eyes. He turned and started toward the stairs.

★ ★ ★

While they waited for the doctor to arrive, Jeff managed to get Sheila into the relative comfort of her own bed.

He fought the urge to ask his wife what had happened, what she had experienced, what she remembered. He could ask later. Or not at all. Although what had happened wasn't their fault, it would have its repercussions. There would be psychiatrists, therapists, counselors, medication — so many things that they had both tried to keep at bay.

Perhaps, he thought, the drugs had helped in some bizarre way. Since she had been kept sedated through most of her ordeal, there might be fewer memories to deal with in the future. But the reality of that might not be fully known for months.

He took a deep breath. They would face it, though, just as they had faced everything else: together.

She stirred next to him, and he searched her face. An odd mix of confusion and distress registered in her gaze.

He debated his best approach. With as normal a voice as he could muster, he said, "I played dress-up with your bonnet earlier tonight." He watched her eyes, thought he saw something behind the bewildered gaze.

Recognition? A tiny flicker of acknowledgment, perhaps? Curiosity? He reached carefully for that thread. "Greer found me. Can you imagine how hard it was for him to keep from laughing?"

She reached out to him then, and he held her close, buried his face in her hair, breathed steadily. They would be okay. They had each other.

It was enough.

RECOMMENDATIONS

FROM JEFFREY TALBOT

Dear Reader,

First and foremost, Sheila's going to be fine. Since I write this letter to you only a couple of weeks after getting her safely back home, I can't say what the next few months will hold. But, with much patience and care from doctors, friends, Greer, and myself, you can rest assured that everything possible is being done.

Many of you wrote to tell me how much you enjoyed the bibliography and webliography I compiled after our last adventure together, so I'm happy to provide you with some new volumes to consider.

Although Sheila's spending less time on the Internet, I've checked her computer for both recently visited and bookmarked sites. I quickly discovered why it's called a Web — I got so caught up in following strand after strand that led to so many sites on antiques, I was afraid of becoming an antique myself before I could check out all of them! But it was interesting, and I've learned nothing if not that the world of antiques is one of constant discovery.

Also, I looked up several sites that have to do with the collectibles showcased in the story you just read. I've listed those in Sheila's webliography, as well.

A few points: 1) Prices of antiques and collectibles will fluctuate for many reasons, including the region where the item is found, the condition it's in, and its current availability on the market; 2) my recommendations are only a scratch on the surface of what's out there, meant simply to whet your appetite and give you a starting place; and 3) people move to new Web addresses just as they move to new street addresses. If you don't locate one of the sites listed, use Jeeves, butler of the Internet (www.askjeeves.com). He's a friend of Greer's.

Speaking of whom, Greer just returned. Since he'll be here with Sheila, I need to make a quick trip down to Blanche's warehouse and sort through some of my inventory. I have a feeling there's more to the old woman's loot than meets the eye. . . .

Till next time,
Jeff Talbot

As I'm compiling this list, fishing collectibles are huge. Here are a few books on the subject:

Old Fishing Lures & Tackle (5th Edition), by Carl F. Luckey (Krause Publications, 1999). Loads of black and white photos, plus a segment of color plates. This book shows photos and provides info on many of the lures found both in Bill Rhodes's collection and in the "poker-chip" tackle boxes brought along on the fishing trip by Kyle Meredith. A great reference book.

Classic Fishing Lures and Tackle: An Entertaining History of Collectible Fishing Gear, by Eric L. Sorenson (Howard Lambert, photographer). This is more than just a lure book, it captures the nostalgic appeal and art of the sport. It's well written and enhanced with excellent photography.

Fishing Lure Collectibles: An Identification and Value Guide to the Most Collectible Antique Fishing Lures, by Dudley Murphy and Rick Edmisten (Collector Books, 2000). Featuring over 1,000 color reproductions as well as descriptions and values of lures, this one's worth a look-see.

The Longest Silence: A Life in Fishing, by Thomas McGuane (Alfred A. Knopf, Inc., 1999). The cover copy of this book's handsome jacket says it best: "Infused with a deep experience of wildlife and the outdoors, dedicated to conservation, reverent and hilarious by turns or at once . . . sets the heart pounding for a glimpse of moving water, and demonstrates what a life dedicated to sport reveals about life." A brilliant work.

If you read *Death Is a Cabaret*, you learned that Gordy Easthope is a diehard fan of Ernest Hemingway. Not surprising then is Gordy's contribution: *Hemingway on Fishing*, edited and with an introduction by Nick Lyons; foreword by Jack Hemingway (The Lyons Press, 2000). This work is the first to collect all of Hemingway's writings about fishing into one volume.

And, of course, the novella I shared with Kyle Meredith: *A River Runs Through It*, by Norman Maclean (University of Chicago, 1976; Pocket Books, 1992). Check out the movie, too. Great casting (I'm talking about the actors, but isn't it interesting how many words we use that have to do with fishing?), including Washington's own Tom Skerritt. Both well done.

The slim volume from which Bill Rhodes's brother read the poem "Romancing the River," is titled *Red Colt Canyon*, by Laurie Wagner Buyer (Music Mountain Press, 1999). I purchased a copy for Sheila, and, before giving it to her, found myself reading the raw and exquisite verses that capture a heedless land and the people who glean an existence from that land.

Vanessa Valentine possesses many books about collecting perfume bottles. The two she suggested I keep on hand are: *The Art of Perfume*, by Christie Mayer Lefkowith (Thames and Hudson, first paperback edition, 1998) and *Miller's Perfume Bottles: A Collector's Guide*, by Madeleine Marsh, with special consultants Linda Bee and Lynda Brine (Octopus Publishing Group Ltd., 1999).

After a chapter covering the formative years of the perfume industry (pre-1900), *The Art of Perfume* offers a decade-by-decade history of the first sixty years of the twentieth century. The visually appealing book — full of color plates — also includes an A–Z of Perfume, which is a sort of encyclopedic guide to perfumers and fashion designers. Personally, I enjoyed the history, which told how events and politics of eras past dictated the designs.

Miller's provides a *wealth* of information in a compact form: where to buy, what to read, collecting tips, and great "Fact File" sidebars.

For valentine enthusiasts, Vanessa suggests two works by Katherine Kreider: *Valentines with Values* (Schiffer Publishing, Ltd., March 1997) and *One Hundred Years of Valentines* (also from Schiffer, February 1999).

Note: When I mentioned these two books to Greer, he told me he'd seen the author and some of her valentine collection featured on Martha Stewart's program, and that she was a charming lady.

The book I studied while on the ferry was *Hidden Treasures: Searching for Masterpieces of American Furniture*, by Leigh Keno and Leslie Keno, with Joan Barzilay Freund (Warner Books, 2000). Many of you will recognize the Keno name from the wildly popular PBS television show, *Antiques Roadshow*. What I know about authenticating furniture masterpieces isn't a patch on what the Kenos knew while they were still in high school. This one was worth the wait.

Reproductions are the bane of the collector and, oftentimes, you can only determine a fake by comparing it to the real McCoy. *The Antique Trader Guide to Fakes & Reproductions*, by Mark Chervenka (Krause Publications, 2001), provides sound information and side-by-side photos of fakes and originals to assist you in identification. (Also, see the *www.repronews.com* listing in the webliography.)

Sam Carver has many books on tools, but the one he most enjoys looking through is *The Art of Fine Tools*, by Sandor Nagyszalanczy (Taunton Press, 1998). Sam keeps it prominently displayed on his coffee table, and I can see why. Many antique tools were more elaborate than the buildings and furniture they helped create, and this edition is generous with its full-color photographs. It includes some good bits (no pun intended) of history, as well. If you appreciate the workmanship, ingenuity, and whimsy of long-ago artisans, then this is the book for you.

Antique Tool Collectors Guide to Value, by Ronald S. Barlow (LW Publishing, 1999), is a new edition of the earlier work, with updated values. Hopefully, your collectibles are worth even more than the values given in this 1999 guide.

Sam also told me that *Grinling Gibbons and the Art of Carving* is a masterpiece, written by master carver David Esterly (Harry N. Abrams, Inc., 1998).

I picked up a fantastic cookbook for Sheila at Seabolts (one of our favorite places to obtain smoked salmon, Sheila orders from them on-line; you'll find them listed in the webliography, below.) The book, *Simply Whidbey*, by Laura Moore and Deborah Skinner, and illustrated by Margaret Livermore (Saratoga Publishers, 1991), contains fabulous regional recipes from Whidbey Island, Washington. As if that weren't enough, it also offers many menus compiled from the recipes, and information on island events — everything from festivals, fairs, and regattas to a mystery weekend.

I haven't discovered a Barbie at a sale in some time, and, after visiting with Sheriff Colleen McIvers, I know why. People are realizing that they're hot. If you're going to collect them, you need to know your stuff. Colleen advises to read up, and recommends *Barbie Bazaar*, the official Barbie Doll Collector's Magazine (a bimonthly publication from Murat Caviale, Inc.). She (Colleen, not Barbie) sent me a copy, which was full of information revealing the lengths scam artists will go to in their attempts to replicate those early dolls (which are currently fetching five figures!).

There are several books on Chris-Craft boats (and Gar Wood boats, as well), so I won't try to influence you one way or the other. But, for the sheer beauty of wooden boats, I will point you toward *Wood Through*

Water: Classic Power Boats, by James W. Ogilvie-Knowles and Justus Hayes (Friedman/Fairfax Publishing, 1999).

The Official Overstreet Price Guide to Comic Books, by Robert M. Overstreet (House of Collectibles, 2002). This annual guide is considered by many to be the bible for this popular collectible. (Thanks to Jon Jordan for the recommendation.)

Note: These statistics were noted in the 2000 film, *Unbreakable*, starring Bruce Willis and Samuel L. Jackson: A single issue ranges in price from $1 to over $140,000, and 172,000 comics are sold in the U.S. every day.

I couldn't bring this segment to a close without directing you to *Coffee Basics: A Quick and Easy Guide*, by Kevin Knox, Julie Sheldon Huffaker (contributor), (John Wiley & Sons, 1996). This guide, written by two industry insiders, lists mail-order sources for the best beans, plus great coffee drink recipes, tasting tips, and a complete coffee taster's glossary.

SHEILA TALBOT'S

WEBLIOGRAPHY

www.antiquelures.com
Hundreds of pages of information, extensive photos. If you're into vintage lures, you've likely made good use of this site. If you're just getting started, allow plenty of time here.

www.barbiecollectibles.com
Official Mattel site for the collectible Barbie. Well-designed, with a wealth of information. Includes an index of Barbie clubs by state.

www.butlersguild.com
Whether you're in the market for a butler, or you want to learn more about this fascinating field of service, you won't go wrong by checking out the Web site for The International Guild of Professional Butlers. (Don't miss the Butler Pantry, an on-line store.)

www.deborahmorgan.com

The author has expanded my segment of her Web site (click "Jeffrey Talbot" in the index) to include more about antiques, additional recipes from Sheila's files, and a better-developed links page, which is now categorized by subject.

www.fishingthenorthwest.com

Includes everything from a list of popular fishing spots to information on lodging, stores, and restaurants near those spots. A well laid-out site, with impressive graphics, too.

Fishing regulations are complicated. Be sure and check out the Washington Department of Fish and Wildlife site at *www.wa.gov/wdfw* for information you'll need prior to making that first cast.

www.kovels.com

Ralph and Terry Kovel have had a passion for antiques for over forty years and have published numerous books about collecting. Their Web site offers extensive databases. The couple also writes a column for *Forbes* magazine, as well as a nationally syndicated newspaper column.

www.marthastewart.com

Both the show and the Web site are popular

in my house. Martha Stewart frequently provides information on collecting, and Sheila enjoys trying out the domestic guru's recipes.

www.nflcc.com

The National Fishing Lure Collectors Club is about more than just lures. It "encompasses every aspect of collecting fishing related tackle and ephemera."

www.oldtools.com

There are many tool collectors clubs and societies. If you're interested, this impressive Web site is a good place to start.

www.perfumebottles.org

Site for the International Perfume Bottle Association. Get info on becoming a member and news about their annual convention. Includes many photos and links to assist in research. The organization publishes the journal *Perfume Bottle Quarterly*.

www.seabolts.com

Seabolts uses locally grown alder wood to smoke salmon in the traditional style of the Pacific Northwest. Located just down the road from Deception Pass, Seabolts has been in business for almost twenty-five years.

www.repronews.com

Web site of the *Antique and Collectors Reproduction News*, a monthly newsletter that provides money-saving tips to keep you on the right track. You can also purchase supplies, such as black lights and invisible ink, to aid in marking your valuables for identification.

www.thomaspink.co.uk

Thomas Pink has great cuff links, which I'm counting on as future vintage pieces for my collection.

Those who noticed the vein of pink that ran through *The Weedless Widow* might appreciate this bit of history from the Thomas Pink Web site: "It's a little-known fact that the phrase 'in the pink' was inspired by our very own Thomas Pink. This legendary Mayfair tailor made his name in the late 18th century, creating hunting coats that were regarded as the finest in the land. If you wore a coat by Mr. Pink, you were definitely on top form — socially, financially, and, of course, sartorially."

www.tullys.com

The folks at Tully's Coffee (which is the exclusive coffee brand of Safeco Field) provide a striking Web site. They offer for purchase a

French-press grind, and if you haven't tried French-pressed coffee, I urge you to check it out. I'm no barista, but I can say that Tully's hasn't steered me wrong yet.

www.vintagewoodworks.com
Spandrels, beadboards, gingerbread, and fretwork can all be found at the site for this Texas-based company. Request a catalog, shop on-line, or check out the bookstore, which lists *dozens* of recommended books on everything from architectural styles to renovation and preservation of historic homes to information on interior elements such as reproduction of historic fabrics, lighting, and wallpapers.

www.washingtonoutdoorwomen.org
Washington Outdoor Women was established in 1997 by the Washington Department of Fish and Wildlife. At the time I checked out this site, the group was offering a number of workshops — from basic fly-tying to big-game hunting.

ABOUT THE AUTHOR

The Weedless Widow is the second novel in Deborah Morgan's antique-lover's mystery series. It follows the critically acclaimed *Death Is a Cabaret,* which won the Reader's Choice Award for Best First Mystery Novel from Chicago's Love is Murder conference, was named a Best Paperback Original of 2001 by *Deadly Pleasures* magazine, was a Top Ten in *Book Sense*'s "Winter Mystery 76," and was one of only two paperback original mysteries to be mentioned in *Publisher's Weekly*'s 2001 debut feature, "The Year in Books." It has been nominated for the Barry Award for Best Paperback Original of 2001.

A transplanted Okie, Morgan now lives in Michigan with her husband, author Loren D. Estleman. One of her favorite pastimes is hunting down treasures to add to her many collections.

Her Web site, www.deborahmorgan.com, has been expanded to include many antiques and collectible links, several additions to Sheila Talbot's recipe box, and current news about the Jeff Talbot series.

We hope you have enjoyed this Large Print book. Other Thorndike, Wheeler or Chivers Press Large Print books are available at your library or directly from the publishers.

For more information about current and upcoming titles, please call or write, without obligation, to:

Publisher
Thorndike Press
295 Kennedy Memorial Drive
Waterville, ME   04901
Tel. (800) 223-1244

Or visit our Web site at:
www.gale.com/thorndike
www.gale.com/wheeler

OR

Chivers Large Print
published by BBC Audiobooks Ltd
St James House, The Square
Lower Bristol Road
Bath BA2 3SB
England
Tel. +44(0) 800 136919
email: bbcaudiobooks@bbc.co.uk
www.bbcaudiobooks.co.uk

All our Large Print titles are designed for easy reading, and all our books are made to last.